"This is a long time coming," Dan said in a husky whisper

He swept her into his arms. "Do you know how often I've thought about it, Jodie, imagined it? But you were always off-limits. Now...what's a kiss between friends?" Dan asked, leaning in close, speaking against her mouth.

The feathery touch was so sexy Jodie moaned again and couldn't tear herself away.

She wanted him more than she'd ever wanted anyone, and her arms snaked up around his neck, her nipples tightening to an almost painful degree as she let herself press against him, seeking some kind of relief.

This can't really be happening, she thought, even as their mouths met and sank into a soft, openmouthed kiss that shook her to her soul.

Blaze

Dear Reader,

Don't you just love friends-to-lovers romances? I do. In *Make Your Move*, Jodie and Dan have been best friends for years, but the qualities that make for a good friendship can be challenging when it comes to romance.

I think smart men are very sexy, and it was fun exploring Dan's sensual side. Jodie is a sexy, confident woman, but she has some demons to face before she can believe in herself enough to commit to Dan. Her "Passionate Hearts" cookies—with an icing that drives men a little crazy—only helps them along.

I love hearing from readers. Please drop me a note at samhunter@samanthahunter.com, or check out my posts to the Blaze Authors Blog (http://blazeauthors.com/blog/) on the third of every month. You can also follow me on Twitter and find me on Facebook.

Enjoy!

Samantha Hunter

Samantha Hunter

MAKE YOUR MOVE

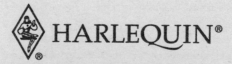

TORONTO • NEW YORK • LONDON
AMSTERDAM • PARIS • SYDNEY • HAMBURG
STOCKHOLM • ATHENS • TOKYO • MILAN • MADRID
PRAGUE • WARSAW • BUDAPEST • AUCKLAND

Recycling programs
for this product may
not exist in your area.

ISBN-13: 978-0-373-79546-8

MAKE YOUR MOVE

ABOUT THE AUTHOR

Samantha Hunter lives in Syracuse, New York, where she writes full-time for Harlequin Books. When she's not plotting her next story, Sam likes to work in her garden, quilt, cook, read and spend time with her husband and their dogs. Most days you can find Sam chatting on the Harlequin Blaze boards at eHarlequin.com, or you can check out what's new, enter contests, or drop her a note at her Web site, www.samanthahunter.com.

Books by Samantha Hunter

Don't miss any of our special offers. Write to us at the following address for information on our newest releases.

Harlequin Reader Service
U.S.: 3010 Walden Ave., P.O. Box 1325, Buffalo, NY 14269
Canadian: P.O. Box 609, Fort Erie, Ont. L2A 5X3

1

"OH, MAN, YOU ARE SO HOT," Jason Kravitz—*Dr.* Jason Kravitz—whispered in Jodie Patterson's ear. His hand rested on her shoulder almost shyly as they walked up the stairs of the old brownstone together.

He wasn't the kind of guy she usually dated, but he was cute in a geeky professor way, with his close-cut brown curls, his serious blue eyes and wire-frame glasses. He'd mentioned playing racquetball, and his physique was nice enough, she was pleased to note.

Mostly, Jodie got a kick out of how attentive and *grateful* he was. A bio engineer at Northwestern, what woman wouldn't be flattered when Jason told her he'd never been out with a woman as sexy as her?

It was an ego stroke, sure, but why not?

I'm gonna rock your world, Dr. Kravitz, she thought with a secretive smile as she impulsively pushed him up against the wall near her apartment and found his lips for a kiss. It was a preview of what she wanted to happen once they were inside the door.

He was a decent kisser, thank God, and from what

she could tell of the boner inside his conservatively cut dress pants, they were in full agreement about how this evening was going to end.

Jodie looked down the hall where a door shut, though she didn't see anyone, and stepped away. She'd lived in this apartment building for six years and knew most of her neighbors. On top of that she was a local business-woman with a reputation to protect. She liked to get wild, but she wasn't stupid.

She felt Jason watching her as if he couldn't bear to take his eyes off her. It was nice, compared to the string of smooth operators she'd dated recently, guys who liked to pretend they were too cool to stroke anyone's ego but their own.

She winked naughtily and crooked her finger. This was going to be *fun*.

They'd had a pleasant enough evening. He'd sprung for a very nice dinner and a show, and she'd cut him some slack on the social graces. After all, Jason was a scientist. A wealthy, nice looking and—she could tell— a well-endowed nerd.

Jodie knew that social dexterity was not the strength of the scientific male. Her best friend and business part-ner Dan Ellison had taught her that. Dan was a good friend and the one guy on earth she could trust and be herself with, but he was still a scientist. A true-blue genius, actually, a teenage college student, Dan was going for his second Ph.D. when Jodie had just hit her sophomore year.

She'd be lying if she didn't admit—at least to herself—that Jason was definitely fulfilling a little fantasy she'd held on to for a while.

Back in the day, more than once, Jodie had thought of what it would be like to sleep with Dan, too. He was sweet, and really good-looking, in spite of his refusal to part with his glasses and somewhat haphazard academic mode of dress. She'd given up buying him beautiful designer shirts and so forth for holidays because he never wore them, though he admired them as gifts. Dan was just…Dan.

Maybe something would have happened in those early days if she'd made a move, but when they opened a business together, the door that led to sex was closed firmly shut. As time went on, she also didn't want to risk destroying the one real relationship she had with a truly decent guy. There was a world full of men to bring home for a night, but really good men were a rare find. Dan was a really good man.

Opening her apartment door, she led Jason in by the tie and when the door shut, she turned on a low light, sliding her coat off and hanging it in the closet before taking his. Their hands touched, and her heartbeat picked up a little. The territory south of her belly button started to get that warm tingle of anticipation that signaled good things on the horizon.

Jodie loved everything about sex. She loved seduction and men's bodies and everything that physical coupling had to offer. It was fun, energizing, and she was very, very good at it. Knowing that gave her a sense of control. She could, with little effort, have any man she wanted. And usually did.

Tonight, that was enhanced by Jason's shy approach. She liked how he wasn't all over her the second the door was shut. He just kept staring at her as if she was the best thing since pink Popsicles.

Jodie grinned. She was an old-fashioned girl in one way: she liked a real man in her bed, not a battery-operated boy toy. Call her a purist, but there really was nothing like the real thing and she didn't settle for facsimiles.

"You make yourself comfortable. I'll be right back," she said with sexy promise in her voice.

Her weekend was off to a perfect start. Sex and fun on Friday night to ease into the weekend, followed by busy Saturday and Sunday mornings at the bakery, and then Sunday afternoon and Monday off to relax and have time to herself. It was a routine honed to perfection over the years. She'd worked hard to get her bake shop, Just Eat It, off the ground. Four years later, now that she was doing well, she'd taken on help and made sure she had time to enjoy life, too.

"Hurry back. Please," he said it so politely, so focused on her and still visibly erect, that she couldn't resist kissing him one more time. She enjoyed it when her lovers were this eager, and begged a little. Taking in his moony-eyed gaze she hoped her science guy wasn't tenderhearted. This was strictly a one-night thing, and she'd make that clear in some gentle way before they hit the sheets. It was better to be honest up front, then everyone could relax and enjoy.

She moved into her bathroom, washed up quickly, spritzing on some perfume and picking a black lace gown from her lingerie closet. Something told her Jason was a traditionalist. She took her hair down from its knot and shook it out, approving of her image in the mirror.

On her way back out to the living room, she saw her cell phone light up on the dresser where she'd left it. She looked down to see who had left her a message.

Dan!

Without hesitation, she picked up the phone and called her voice mail to check.

"Jodie? You there? It's me, Dan," he said in the message, as if she wouldn't recognize his voice. "I'm back a few days early, and the guy subletting from me isn't out of the apartment until Sunday. I'm at a hotel, but call me on my cell if you want to have dinner or get together. I'll be up late, so don't worry."

She smiled, holding on to the phone for a second. She hadn't realized until she heard his voice how much she missed him.

Dan was a very busy guy. Since college, he'd been in high demand as a speaker and guest lecturer. He still did that now that he was a professor at the university—when he wasn't working on government contracts associated with the department's high-security experiments. When someone had a gift like Dan's, everyone seemed to want a piece of him. He'd been teaching less in recent years, away more often than not, so they didn't hang out as regularly as they had in the old days, although they tried to spend time together in between his varied engagements.

Those speaking engagements had always paid quite

well, as did his many publications. As his college years had been completely funded by a scholarship, he'd been accumulating quite the bank account since he was young.

Not so for Jodie, who'd worked her way up and, even with her scholarship, had worked all through college to be able to afford the necessities. However, Dan was never arrogant about his accomplishments, and he never acted as if he was better than everyone else. Quite the opposite, when she'd met him, he was a bit of a loner.

They became friends, and eventually he became her silent partner, bankrolling the bakery at the beginning. He'd also developed their "secret ingredient"—a cookie icing that held pheromone additives that enhanced female sexual attractiveness. In other words, eat a cookie or two with that icing on it, and any woman would attract men that she was also attracted to, releasing the pheromone along with the usual chemical something-or-others that all combined to create lust.

Dan had explained how it all worked—in painful detail—and Jodie had listened, though she only understood about five words of what he was saying.

Dan's invention was the thing that had put her on the map of the Chicago specialty foods scene with her Passionate Hearts cookies—for adults only, of course. After a few write-ups in food and women's magazines, she was even considering a Web site and online sales.

To do that, she'd have to hire another baker, but she needed to make sure she was hiring the right person, and had been stalling. When it came to her business, she was nowhere near as daring as she was in her social life. She'd been meaning to ask Dan his opinion; maybe he would like to conduct interviews with her.

Jodie was a social butterfly and Dan was more solitary. She dated a lot of guys and was sexually and socially adventurous, enjoying going out with her friends and traveling when she could. Her female friendships were the cornerstone of her social life, though. After growing up with a dominating father and watching her mother suffer for it, as did Jodie, she had no desire to attach herself to any man for longer than a night.

Men were just for sex, and none of them seemed to mind.

Dan was the exception to the rule, in a platonic way. He'd never made a move on her, and for that, she was grateful. He was as dedicated to work as she was, and that, as well as their college friendship, was their glue.

Dan had dated three women that she knew of, one in grad school and two later, fairly seriously, but he was ultimately married to his work. Not many women could put up with his frequent absences and the times when, even though he was sitting right there with you, his mind was off solving some problem.

The women he dated tended to be as smart as he was. Jodie knew she didn't compete in that area. She wasn't stupid, but she was hardly on Dan's level when it came to brain power.

Dialing quickly, she called his cell, which she knew by rote.

"Jodie," he greeted her warmly on the second ring. The same surge of comfort and happiness overcame her, too, hearing his voice.

"Dan, I'm sorry, I just got your message. I was, uh—" she said, glancing toward the front room where Jason waited.

"Out on a date, yes. It's Friday night. I'm sorry. I remembered just as soon as I left the message. I'm a little bleary on what day it is. They've all blended together lately. Who's the lucky fella?"

"Um, just a guy. Actually, um, he's..."

"There. I understand," he said easily. "You didn't need to call me right back."

She smiled, shaking her head at how he finished her thoughts. They'd been friends for that long. Suddenly the sexy night she'd had planned with Jason didn't seem so exciting.

"It's been a while," she said, letting the black gown fall to the floor and yanking open a drawer, grabbing some underwear, yoga pants and a tank top. She dressed as she was talking. "How long are you home?"

"I'm teaching, so I'll be here for the year this time. Wanted to get home a few weeks before the semester started to get ready. Didn't I tell you before I left?"

"Nope," she said, though there wasn't any blame in her tone. She was used to him forgetting details like that.

"Listen, there's no hurry. Go enjoy your date."

She paused, a little ding of hurt around her breastbone. Didn't he want to see her, too? But he sounded tired. That had to be it. Dan didn't do subterfuge. If he didn't want to see her, he'd say so.

"Are you okay?"

"Braincloud," he said wearily, and she grinned,

understanding immediately. "Braincloud" was the inside joke they shared after watching the movie *Joe Versus the Volcano* to describe the complete fog and exhaustion Dan suffered when he came out of his work-saturated life.

Dan worked with such intensity. In college, he'd get so stuck in a project that he'd forget to eat, sleep, or to even leave his room. Once, he'd stayed in his room for so long working out a problem that the people in adjoining rooms thought something was terribly wrong and called her, the dorm student rep, to check it out.

He'd barely noticed when she'd gotten security to open the door and they found him amid a forest of books and papers, his attention completely tuned to his work. He hadn't eaten for two days, and Jodie had taken it upon herself from then on to bring him food when he was working.

Eventually, it became a ritual. She'd come to his lab or his dorm room with food and they'd share a break. She made him laugh, and he helped her get through three years of required math for her business degree. She baked him things all the time, and it had been his idea for her to open a bakery.

When other guys were trying to find the best way to get into her pants, Dan had just enjoyed her company and never asked for more. When she'd been turned down by one bank after another to start her business, having a weak credit history and no rich parents to back her up, Dan had stepped up and loaned her the money. He'd had plenty saved and had been collecting money from patents and other work for years.

It paid to be a child genius, and he was more than generous in sharing with Jodie, no questions asked. Later, when he developed the icing formula, she signed him on as partner. Even though she had been paying back his loan, it was only fair that he share in her profits.

She'd been a little surprised, but pleased, when he accepted.

"You haven't eaten, have you?" she said, knowing.

"I'll call room service, promise. Listen, you have someone waiting—you have fun," he said, starting to hang up.

"Wait. This guy, you know, it isn't important. I don't think we were clicking anyway," she said, with her fingers crossed, just in case. "I haven't seen you in forever. I'll be there in an hour with a pizza. Where are you?"

He told her, and she called in the order for their favorite deep dish, wondering how she'd let Jason down easily. It wasn't fair, getting the guy all worked up and then fleeing the scene, but she wasn't in the mood anymore. She'd make it up to him another time.

2

"JODIE, DEAR, I *must* have more of those cookies!"

"Coming, Mrs. Mitchell!" Jodie grabbed the tray of cookies, just frosted, and headed back out to the counter. Outside the window, people bustled by on Wells St. in Chicago's Old Town neighborhood.

She'd been up late the night before catching up with Dan and didn't expect to be handling the bakery alone this Saturday morning. Ginger's babysitter had let her down, so she had to make other arrangements and wasn't here yet.

"Oh! And they're fresh!" Mrs. Mitchell exclaimed as she eyed the new sugar cookies, shaped as hearts and decorated red with the secret frosting recipe that Jodie couldn't make fast enough.

There'd been some question in local blogs and food columns if the cookies were just a marketing gimmick or the real deal, and Jodie let the conversation flourish. Everyone liked to speculate about her "special formula" or whether it was simply a self-fulfilling prophecy. After all, who had ever heard of pastry that attracted the attention of the opposite sex? But the doubting Thomases just drove more business in her direction, more people wanting to see if they were for real.

In Jodie's experience, she knew that the effect—for adult women, anyway—was very real.

Dan had explained that the pheromone extract that he used, a harmless celery derivative, reacted only with adult women's body chemistry. The woman had to be attracted to someone in the first place, for the "boosters" in the cookie icing to even take effect. So it wasn't as if strange men would be lusting after anyone.

After much testing and licensing she was confident about serving it, and had received no complaints from customers. Men and young people would only get a sugar rush from the frosting, but Jodie found that keeping the cookies in a special "adult only" case behind the counter increased the mystique, and the sales.

"They are. How many would you like?"

"I'll take all of them."

Jodie gaped for a moment. Her special cookies weren't inexpensive. If Mrs. Mitchell bought all of these, Jodie would be out of cookies for the day. She'd have to rush to bake more, or turn away unhappy customers later.

"All of them? They don't freeze well, Mrs. Mitchell," she said. It was hard to imagine turning down a sale, but still…

"Oh, they don't?" her customer asked with some disappointment.

"Well, they would taste fine, but the freezing will reduce their *effect*," Jodie said with a wink, though she had no idea if that was true.

"Oh, then, we can't have that. What would be the point? Just give me a half-dozen then. I sneak two every afternoon with coffee. Rupert hasn't been this attentive in years."

"Glad to hear it," Jodie said, smiling, relieved.

Working the morning shift alone had been hectic enough as it was without worrying about having to do extra baking. Jason had been leaving messages, and she meant to call him back, but the coffee delivery had been late and between covering the counter and working in the kitchen, she'd been running around like a chicken with its head cut off.

She put the cookies carefully in a white box, humming to the music playing over the speaker system as she wrapped the box with her signature red ribbon displaying the name of the shop.

"Here you go, Mrs. Mitchell. That will be thirty dollars even."

The middle-aged lady handed over the money happily and with a big smile. "Thank you, Jodie."

"Don't eat them all at once. You don't want Rupert losing all control," Jodie warned playfully as two more customers walked in the door.

"Oh, no, he's on blood pressure medication, though the extra exercise *is* good for him," she answered with a girlish giggle, walking back out onto the street.

Jodie shook her head, chuckling. She settled into the routine rhythm of her morning, waiting on customers, refilling the display case, cleaning as she went and making up new specials signs and racks. She had things more or less under control when Ginger finally walked in, looking stressed to the teeth.

"Hi—everything okay with Anna?"

"Yes. I'm so sorry I'm late."

"No worries."

"Mom came over, so I had to wait for her to arrive. She's watching Anna at my place, but Anna didn't want me to leave. She's having some serious separation anxiety issues, and I couldn't leave Mom to deal with her screaming. It's enough that she's probably noticing all of the housekeeping that I haven't been able to do lately," Ginger said grumpily.

"Is she okay?"

"Mom? Fine."

"No, Anna."

"Ah, well…that's another story."

Ginger looked worried as she hung her light jacket on the hook near the entry to the kitchen, grabbing her blue apron and tying it around her trim waist.

Jodie couldn't help feeling sorry for Ginger, the only one of her friends with a child, and never wanted to find herself in the same situation. Ginger worked two jobs to support herself and her daughter, freelancing as a personal trainer in addition to working at the bakery. As Jodie's only full-time employee, she gave her as many hours as she could, still she couldn't imagine how stressful it must be to raise a child alone.

"Scott again?" Jodie guessed.

"Right the first time. He popped back up last weekend, and it's so confusing for Anna. He gets an attack of guilt a few times a year and decides to ease his conscience with a visit, then disappears again. When Anna was younger, it wasn't such an issue, but now… it's starting to show at school. She's acting out, and it's playing havoc with my life as well as hers."

Jodie murmured sympathetically and offered a hug. Though she tried not to spend too much time thinking about her less than ideal childhood in a working-class neighborhood of Philly, where her dad had been a mechanic and her mom a lunch lady at the elementary school, Jodie couldn't help the memories sneaking up on her now and then.

Don Patterson had been an asshole of tremendous proportions, constantly expecting perfection, even from a six-year-old. Jodie couldn't remember ever receiving a kind word from her father, and she'd gotten out of town as fast and as far away as she could when she'd graduated high school. He'd wanted her to stay home, to go to a local school, but she'd resisted.

He'd died when she was in college, and she hadn't bothered going home for the funeral. For that reason, her mother hadn't spoken to her since then, either. She didn't lose a lot of sleep over it, since her mother hadn't ever defended her, but just let her father take over.

Jodie shook her head, blowing out a breath and offering Ginger a cranberry muffin. "Get some coffee, sit, and decompress. Things are slow for the moment."

"Thanks. You're one in a million, Jodie."

Jodie patted her on the shoulder and wiped the fingerprints from the fronts of the glass display cases more vigorously. In her experience, men rarely cared if they stomped on your heart or ruined your life in the process of getting what they wanted. Ginger and Anna were two more examples of that.

Still, women had more choices now, and Jodie always congratulated herself and her friends for opting to be independent career women, and she wanted to support Ginger in doing the same, if she could.

She didn't hate men because of her father, God, no. Men were luscious. They were fun and wonderful, but a girl couldn't let herself get in too deep. Jodie never did. Guys were drawn to her voluptuous thirty-eight-C build and her long brown hair and blue eyes since she could remember.

"Whoa, hottie alert," Ginger almost purred as a guy ran by the bakery, drawing both of their gazes in appreciation. He stopped mid-stride and turned around.

"That's what I'm talking about," Jodie said admiringly, to herself, though Ginger overhead and nodded.

"Uh-oh, he's coming in!" Ginger laughed as he approached the door.

Jodie shushed her employee with a grin and greeted the guy, discreetly admiring his sleek runner's build. "Can I help you?"

He walked up to the counter, smiling. All blond and tan, he was probably a few years younger than Jodie's thirty-two, closer to Ginger's twenty-seven.

"Sure. You have anything whole grain? And some water?"

"Water is in the case, and we have some fresh bran muffins that are cooling from the oven. Ginger would be happy to get one for you—or more than one?"

"No," he said, smiling in Ginger's direction. "One is fine."

Ginger's head snapped up from where she'd been admiring him from the waist down through the glass case, her cheeks flushing prettily. Their handsome customer didn't seem to mind at all as he took in her curly red hair and pale complexion.

"Uh, sure. Just a minute," she stammered, and disappeared.

"She'll be right back," Jodie promised with a smile. Ginger needed a boost, and waiting on a cute guy was just the ticket. Jodie made herself scarce when Ginger returned, reorganizing some cakes she had organized five minutes before at the far end of the display case.

To her amazement, Ginger finished the sale without even getting the guy's name. When he left, Jodie popped up and looked at her assistant squarely, hands on hips.

"Ginger, why didn't you flirt a little? He was into you."

"Why do you think that?"

"He asked you about every muffin we have on the board, even the sugary ones, and all the ingredients in this one—and he was staring at your boobs. He also mentioned thinking he'd seen you at the gym. He was doing everything he could to get you to connect. You just handed him his receipt and told him to have a good day."

"Yeah, I guess," Ginger said grumpily, shrugging. "I must be getting rusty. I haven't been with anyone since Scott."

Jodie's mouth dropped open. "Seriously? That's been almost two years."

Ginger leveled her a look. "Jodie, I work two jobs and I'm a mom. I've trained myself to not notice hot guys coming on to me because I don't have time. Besides, once they find out I have a kid they're not so interested."

"You deserve some grown-up fun," Jodie insisted, not liking the loneliness she saw in her friend's eyes.

Ginger smiled, but it wasn't a happy smile. "I know you like to love 'em and leave 'em, but I don't feel right doing one-night stands anymore. I have Anna to consider. Don't you ever want something more permanent?"

"No way. And 'permanent' is what got you Scott in the first place, if you remember. A one-night stand is exactly what you need. Besides, I never love any of them, I only fu—"

"Jodie!" Ginger cut her off before she could finish her sentence, laughing and turning pink.

Jodie shrugged, grinning, happy she could lighten up the mood. "I'm just saying it would be good for you. I could take Anna for an overnight and you could go out to play. He must enjoy working out. You have something in common from the start. Maybe you could find something more interesting to do on the exercise equipment than exercise, you know?"

"You are just bad." Ginger peered at her, taking a sip of her coffee. "Well, he's gone now, anyway, so it's a nonissue. For what it's worth, I don't buy your 'I don't fall in love' routine. You just haven't found the right guy. One of these days he'll come along and you're not even going to know what hit you. Then you'll see my side of things."

"Doubt it."

"Mark my words. One of these days, Jodie Patterson is going to fall and fall hard. I can't wait. You deserve a good guy."

"Yeah, well, we all do, but there are precious few of them out there."

Ginger murmured agreement to that and went back to her task.

Jodie was amazed that Ginger's romantic illusions still held after what she'd been through. Jodie had figured out in high school what guys were interested in, and it seemed so obvious.

She was diverted from her thoughts when Jason walked in the door. She looked at him in surprise, and then realized she'd never responded to any of his morning calls or text messages.

"Hi, Jodie," he said quietly, as he approached her. Ginger wiggled her eyebrows and discreetly left them alone.

"Hi Jason," she said, putting on her prettiest smile. "I'm really sorry about last night."

"Me, too."

She walked out around the case to where he stood. "I was hoping you'd let me make it up to you."

"I wasn't sure you wanted to. When I didn't hear from you, I thought I was getting the brush-off." He grinned crookedly. "I figured guys like me weren't much your style, so I didn't blame you, and wanted to come by and say no hard feelings."

"Nonsense," she said, reaching up for a quick kiss, glancing sideways to make sure no customers were coming in the door. "Let's make some plans tonight. I'm off in a few hours." She was breaking her weekend routine, but she kind of owed the guy. That, and she really wanted to get laid. Due to work and other obligations it had been a few weeks, and she was overdue.

She'd had a great time with Dan the night before, chowing down on double-stuffed pizza and talking into the night. Now that she'd spent some time with him, she felt good as new, and ready to get back to normal.

"Absolutely," he said, leaning in for another kiss.

She averted his kiss as the bell over the door rang. She dusted off her apron, putting a few feet between them as she turned to greet her customer, and instead saw Dan walk in the door. Dressed in his usual jeans, sneakers, white T-shirt and the tweed jacket he'd worn since she could remember, he squinted behind his thick glasses, adjusting to the light inside. He broke into a smile when he saw her.

"Hey you." She greeted him with pleasure at the surprise, closing the distance and hugging him without restraint. For a moment she completely forgot about Jason, unworried about being seen because, well, it was just Dan.

IT WAS AS IF someone flicked a switch in Dan's world and the light came on. That's the feeling he always had whenever he was with Jodie. Bright and warm, like the incandescent bulbs that were hot to the touch and bathed you in a natural glow.

She'd spent time with him the night before, bringing some completely unhealthy and delicious food for them to share, and he'd talked more than he ever did to anyone. That had always been the case.

"I thought you'd be sleeping off three months of work still," she said, teasing him lightheartedly. Dan liked it that she knew him so well. He knew her, too.

For instance, he knew that she very likely had a date at her apartment last night. He knew that if he called, she'd probably cancel it to come see him and send the guy home. He wanted to feel ashamed of that, but he didn't.

"I recovered pretty quickly. New diet. I've been exercising more, as well. It was the only way to stay sane in D.C. We worked nearly 24/7."

"You didn't say much. Is it one of those things where you could tell me about it, but then you'd have to kill me?"

"More like if I told you about it, you'd probably be bored to death," he responded, grinning. Banter with Jodie was always easy.

"I've barely seen daylight for ninety days," he admitted, keeping one arm slung loosely around her as they turned into the shop.

"Poor l'il genius," she teased, and he laughed.

In truth, the work had been fascinating, but she was right, he couldn't talk about it. Dan wondered if Jodie would see him differently—if he'd be sexier or more attractive to her—if she knew that his work had probably helped save millions of lives.

It was irrational to speculate, but since he'd left D.C.

he'd had only one thing on his mind: seeing Jodie. Usually he forgot everything when he was working, but it seemed that this time, he'd been more distracted. He'd thought of calling her while he was there, but security procedures prohibited it.

He was simply dealing with the usual disorientation he always experienced after an intense project, feeling grumpy and disconnected for the past few days. He hadn't felt as though the world was right again until Jodie showed up at his door last night. It might be irrational, but it was true.

As they'd talked into the night, he'd experienced something a little more intense than friendship. It wasn't the first time—he'd repressed an attraction to Jodie for years—but she'd been on his mind more than not lately. If he'd found it difficult to leave Chicago three months ago, it was because he'd be away from her. Those thoughts and feelings were exactly why he'd decided he had to go. But he hadn't been interested in being with anyone since.

Three months was a long time to go without a bed partner, even for him. Physical release was part of maintaining a healthy mind, and he'd always enjoyed sex when the opportunity presented itself. He looked at her again, paying more attention to the soft swell of her breasts, the grace of her neckline.

As they stood close, he closed his eyes and used a quick meditation technique he'd learned directly from Tibetan monks to will his very sex-starved body not to respond to the scent of her pretty hair.

She was his friend. She was his business partner. He shouldn't be sporting a woody from hugging her.

When she kissed him on the cheek, knocking his glasses sideways, they laughed and she disentangled herself, letting him set his vision right.

And she *was* a vision, all pink cheeked and blue eyed. She didn't see him as anything other than a friend, never had, never would. He'd wished for more from time to time, but had discounted it as a random urge. Except that it kept coming back. Now, in their thirties, his mind was turning more seriously to the possibility.

"Dan? Dan? Yoo-hoo. You in there?"

He smiled, embarrassed. Sometimes she could take him back to being a virginal seventeen-year-old. Other times he wanted to show her just how much he knew about a woman's body and how it worked.

"Sorry. Still getting back into the swing of things. You know how it is."

She rolled her eyes, taking his hand. "I do. Brain-cloud."

"Braincloud," he repeated agreeably. Though he was really clear as a bell, focused intently on her soft hand in his.

Damn, her skin was like silk. He knew it was simply due to the high moisture content of her cells, good genes and proper care of her epidermis to prevent damage from sun and loss of oils, but none of that reduced the effect of her feminine fingers lightly clasping his. He had to close his eyes again, almost tripping as she pulled him across the front of the store, to try to tamp his body's response.

"Dan, I want you to meet Jason. You guys are both…" she said, drifting off as she saw his reaction, and Jason's. Dan hadn't been aware of anyone in the store but Jodie.

"Dr. Kravitz," Dan said coolly.

"Dr. Ellison," Jason returned in the same tone. "Back so soon?"

Dan's smiled quirked. "I made it clear I'd be back for the start of the new semester," he said with a smile. "After all, I am department chair this year, as well."

Dan loved teaching and hadn't had as much time for it in recent years, but this time he'd limited his time away over the summer. It was time to start making some changes. For over a decade, he'd been at the service of whoever wanted to make use of his intellect, but now he was going to start doing the things that made him happy. Teaching. Working in his lab. Being with friends.

Being with Jodie.

He also loved being at the university, and while most of his colleagues were a pleasure to work with, Jason Kravitz was a snake. More than that, he was a bad scientist, someone who worked only for his own profit and who had displayed other unethical behaviors, at least from what Dan had heard through the grapevine. Jason worked nearby, and Dan was grateful that he only ever saw Jason in passing or at departmental meetings. Though, since he'd asked to chair the department this year—which, in part, meant supervising courses, professors and projects—he would be seeing more of him.

Dan was a peaceful guy. He believed in live and let

live, and he liked most people he came into contact with, but Jason had always rubbed him the wrong way.

So what was he doing here, and why was Jodie introducing them?

A quick deduction punched him in the gut...Jason was the guy Jodie was with the night before.

Dan had to bite his tongue, hard.

She deserved so much better, but he'd never been able to get her to believe it. The one time he'd tried talking her out of sleeping with a guy he knew at school was the only serious argument they ever had. They hadn't spoken for a month. She said he was judging her. He wasn't.

Jason had a reputation in their small academic circle as a womanizer. He bragged about using the popular image of science geeks in the media to get women into bed at conferences and bars. There were also rumors about him having affairs with lab assistants and his advisees—clearly unethical behavior, though nothing was ever proven.

"Uh, you two know each other?" Jodie asked.

"Yes," they responded simultaneously, in the same monotone laced with dislike.

"We work in the same department at Northwestern, but manage different labs. Our offices are on the same floor," Dan clarified. "What are you doing here, Jason?"

"Visiting with Jodie. We've been dating. I had no idea you knew each other. She never mentioned you," Jason said casually, putting a hand on Jodie's shoulder.

Dating? As in, more than Jodie's usual one-night

flings? Jodie had told him the guy she was with the night before wasn't someone she was all that interested in, which was why she'd cut the date short to come see him. Jason certainly made it sound like they had more going on.

Dan didn't have a good mantra for this particular situation. Never being inclined to violence, he'd never had to ask the monks how to avoid the urge to slam his fist into someone's face.

"We've only been on one date," Jodie corrected gently, smiling at them both. Dan hoped his relief wasn't too evident.

Still, had they slept together? Was she so impressed she was agreeing to see Jason again? He was coming here, to her workplace, to flirt? To *seduce* her?

Dan saw all shades of red though he was hoping his exterior didn't betray his thoughts. Thinking of Jodie with Jason made his highly developed mind turn caveman.

"We were out last night," Jodie said, "but I didn't feel well so we called it a night early."

Her eyes met his, and Dan took it for the hint that it was. Don't tell him about last night. It made him feel better—and worse. She'd blown Jason off for him, but she didn't want Jason knowing that.

"We're going to more than make up for it later," Jason said, sticking the knife in a little deeper.

"Later?" Dan said without thinking.

"I wanted to make up my date with Jason, since I had to beg off last night," she explained, her cheeks turning pink.

He'd stopped Jodie from sleeping with Jason. Maybe he was lucky. Or maybe not, since it sounded like she was intent on seeing him again.

Dan suddenly realized he hadn't said a word, standing there like an idiot, and he caught the knowing glint in Jason's eyes as he bent down and kissed Jodie—on the cheek.

"Well, I—I have to go, Jodie," Jason stammered enough to sound shy and a little unsure. "See you later?"

The bastard, Dan thought, curling his fingers into fists as he observed Jason's naive act. Women really fell for this?

Jodie sparked up. "Oh, wait! I can't—I forgot I already have plans tonight."

Dan's relief was almost palpable.

"How about tomorrow night?" she said instead, and relief went out the window. He wasn't used to this emotional roller coaster.

"Sure," Jason agreed.

Dan ground his teeth. Jodie wasn't inexperienced with men. Didn't she see the predatory gleam in the guy's eye? That he was only using her. That he was lying through his teeth? Dan then reminded himself that she probably didn't care. As much as he loved Jodie, he knew she wasn't much of a romantic. She was used to sex as sport, he thought sadly.

"I'll see you then," Jodie said with a friendly smile.

When Jason left, he slid Dan a covert glance that was completely galling.

Trouble was, there was no way to tell Jodie that Jason

was a dog without sounding jealous, needy, or causing the same problem they'd had years ago when he'd tried to interfere. Jodie didn't like anyone telling her what to do, not even him. She'd had enough of that from her father. She wouldn't listen to Dan if he warned her off Jason; in fact, it might even make Jason more appealing.

"Dan, you okay? You look like you should sit down."

He shook his head, smiling. "I'm fine. Tired. Lost in thought."

"C'mon. Probably your blood sugar bottoming out, in which case, you are in the right place. Let's get a snack and say hi to Ginger."

She took his arm in hers and he found he wanted to pull her in, to gather her in close and protect her and make sure no man, certainly not a man like Jason Kravitz, laid one hand on her. Ever.

Instead, he walked with her to the kitchen, listening to her chatter about the bakery. Ginger welcomed him cheerfully. All the while, as they talked about D.C., the bakery and what was happening in Chicago, his mind was working out his problem. He could hear himself conversing with Jodie and Ginger but his mind was miles away.

He had less than a day to prevent Jodie from making a terrible choice. One day to keep her out of Jason's bed.

Dan's eyes landed on the Passionate Hearts cookies. In less than a minute, his problem was solved.

3

THE NEXT MORNING, Jodie found herself in a replay of the day before.

Hustling back and forth from the kitchen, she looked at the clock and wondered where Ginger had gotten to. Again, she'd popped out to pick up Anna from Sunday school, but it was nearly eleven and it shouldn't take her this long to get there and back. They were only open until one, but Ginger usually covered the counter while Jodie set up for Monday in the kitchen. Now, nothing was done and she wasn't ready for her date with Jason, either.

Peevishness turned into concern. Ginger was not unreliable. Something had to be wrong. Jodie, who didn't give into the impulse to worry too often, was very worried now.

She should call and cancel with Jason. She really didn't want to give up her cherished Sunday night at home anyway. For whatever reason, her interest in taking him to bed had waned dramatically. She knew she was just seeing him out of guilt, for having walked out on him Friday night. Usually, when it came to guys, she didn't do guilt.

Looking up as the door opened, she hoped it was Ginger but instead saw the handsome runner from the day before. He stopped in the doorway, checking around a bit, and then focused on her, smiling.

"Hi."

"Hi. Can I help you?"

He smiled in a slightly bashful way. "I hope so. First, I'm not a stalker or anything, but I was hoping that other girl, the one who waited on me yesterday, might be here?"

Jodie quirked an eyebrow. "Why?"

"She was...cute, if a little on the serious side, but I was hoping maybe she'd meet me for a coffee or something. I wanted to ask her. I'm Robert. Robert Castilla."

"Hi Robert," Jodie said, moving out from behind the glass case and standing with her arms crossed, regarding him closely. It wasn't her place to give him information about Ginger. That didn't mean she couldn't give information to Ginger about him. "What kind of work do you do?"

"I'm a physical therapist at St. Mary's Hospital. Been there for four years," he answered easily. That explained the shape he was in, the care he took with that lithe, athletic body. It also said he liked to help people, and he probably wasn't wealthy, but money wasn't everything.

"Sox or Cubs?"

"Sox," he said immediately, maybe a little hopefully. It wasn't completely a fair question, since while she was a Cubs fan, Jodie knew Ginger didn't care a whit about baseball, being a devout Blackhawks fan.

"Do you like kids?" Jodie asked, remembering how Ginger said guys lost interest as soon as they found out she had a kid.

"Sure. Kids are cool. I work with a lot of them."

"My friend...she's a single mom."

"I admire that. My sister is a single mother. Hard to believe someone that hot is a mom, though," he said with a crooked grin, and Jodie's heart warmed.

She smiled. "Okay, listen Robert, I can't speak for her, but I can tell her you stopped by, and if you want to leave her your number or stop by Monday when she's here all day, that's fine. In fact, you can have coffee here, on the house," Jodie added, making it both easy for him and safe for Ginger.

He appeared relieved to have passed muster but shook his head. "I have to work an extra shift this week, covering vacations, but I'll leave her my number, and could you let her know I was here?"

"Sure."

He wrote down his name, phone number and e-mail in strong, male script. Jodie took it, putting it up on their bulletin board in the back. This would be good for Ginger, in spite of her worries.

Jodie glanced at the clock and realized she would be working the ovens for the afternoon. She hadn't eaten since breakfast, either. She grabbed a few Passionate Hearts, as they were right in front of her, and walked to the back to get some milk.

Her pheromones could use some action, and maybe

she could tell Jason they'd stay in, order some takeout, and she could work off this nervous energy that was building inside her. They'd both get what they wanted, and that would be that. She knew there wouldn't be a third date.

Although having him at her place for the evening could give him ideas, she thought, munching and sipping the ice-cold milk. If she was going to do it, maybe better to go out. A quickie at a restaurant that had handy coat closets sounded fun. She could find some darkened corner where she could sneak her science geek away.

The idea had merit, she noticed, her nipples hardening a little as she closed her eyes and thought about what she and Dan could do in the dark corner of a crowded little coat closet, other patrons passing by only a few feet away.

She almost dropped her half-eaten cookie to the floor. *Dan?* No…she meant Jason.

She was getting her scientists mixed up. Peeking down at her traitorous nipples, she said sternly to herself, "Stop that. This thing you have about Dan is so not going to happen!"

Finishing her cookies, she took a deep breath and headed over to the counter, surprised to see the object of her minifantasy had just walked through the door of the shop.

"Hey Jodie—how's it going?" Dan said, smiling. He didn't usually come by the store so often, not that she was complaining.

He seemed casual enough, but something was different. She narrowed her eyes, trying to figure it out.

"Surprised to see you in here again so soon," she said lightly, studying him and feeling her cheeks heat, no doubt because a few minutes earlier she'd been thinking about the two of them groping each other in close quarters.

"I was out for a Sunday morning walk, and wanted something sweet," he said, looking at her so closely her cheeks turned warm. What the heck was going on?

He looked so...*hot*. Dan was always good-looking in his Clark Kent kind of way, but when had it ever hit her that he was really sexy? As in, *come over here behind the counter baby and I'll give you something sweet* sexy?

She cleared her throat. "Well, we're pretty picked over from the Sunday morning rush, but you're still partner in this place. Help yourself," she said, trying to smile, crossing her arms casually over her traitorous breasts.

Dan walked behind the counter, perusing the case. He moved to where she stood, and she inhaled his cologne—since when did Dan wear cologne?

"You—you're wearing cologne," she said lamely.

"Yeah. Do you like it?"

If the way she was suddenly aching in particular spots meant anything, then yes, she could say she did.

"It's unusual for you," she replied, her voice breathless. Maybe she was allergic to the scent, she realized, her mind feeling a bit fuzzy.

What the heck was happening here? She stepped away, but Dan traveled down the length of the case with her. He didn't pay any attention to her. He simply glanced through all the goodies as if deciding what he wanted.

She knew what *she* wanted, unfortunately, squeezing her thighs together beneath the apron, a small moan escaping her lips.

Then he straightened and faced her.

"You okay?"

"Yeah, uh, I didn't sleep well last night," she lied.

There was a hint of mischief in his eyes, and his sandy-brown hair looked...soft. She itched to touch it.

"You'd never know it. You look gorgeous today. As usual," he said in a low, sexy tone that seemed to rumble through her core.

"Thanks. You seem...different," she said, again lacking for words as lust fogged her brain.

Dan, Dan, Dan, her mind yelled, as if trying to get her lust-saturated brain to recognize how wrong this was. They were friends. They'd never looked at each other this way. She could tell by the way his hazel irises darkened, the pupils expanding, that he was responding to her, too.

The cookies. She'd eaten two of the cookies, and she was already missing sex over the last few weeks. Obviously, it was starting to affect her.

Him, too.

He stared at her deeply, his eyes hungry, as if he wanted to pounce on her and bite her...in the best possible way.

"Oh, no," she whispered, backing up and finding only the wall behind her.

"What? What's wrong?"

"It's the cookies, Dan, I had some cookies…that's all. If you're feeling a little, uh, turned on, that's why. It's not me. It's the cookies," she babbled desperately as he stepped in closer.

Oh my, she thought, when something very prominent in his pants brushed her thigh. Her insides melted, quickly soaking her panties in sheer desire.

He reached up, pulled the scarf from her head and let her hair fall loose.

"I think it's you, Jodie. Remember, the cookies only have an effect if you are releasing attractor pheromones of your own in the first place. The cookies are only an enhancement of what your body is already feeling," he said on a hushed breath, his lips close but not touching hers.

"Oh," was all she could manage, focused on his mouth.

"This is a long time coming," he said in a husky, masculine whisper. "Do you know how many times I've thought about it, imagined it? But you were always off-limits."

"Still am. You, too." She was trying painfully to get him to see reason, though she really wanted him to push her up against the wall and do whatever he desired. "We're partners. Friends," she said, desperately.

"Yes. What's a kiss between friends?" he asked, leaning in closer, speaking against her mouth. The feathery touch was so sexy she moaned again and couldn't tear herself away.

She wanted him more than she'd ever wanted anyone, and her arms snaked themselves up around his neck, her nipples tightening to an almost painful degree as she let herself press against him, seeking some kind of relief.

This can't really be happening, she thought, even as their mouths met and sank into a soft, openmouthed kiss that shook her to her soul.

She threaded her fingers into his hair, felt him take his glasses off even as they kissed, one arm coming around her back, the other sliding seductively behind her head where he held her steady. Without warning, he changed the kiss from a gentle seduction to a full-on penetration of his tongue into her mouth, rubbing against hers, opening her so completely that she couldn't help but shudder from head to toe.

Jodie had been kissed by a lot of men. A lot. She wasn't sure any man had ever kissed her this deeply, this thoroughly, or for this long.

He took his time, explored every bit of soft, wet skin. When he sucked her tongue into his mouth, moving the hand on her back to her breast, she gasped, a sudden orgasm rolling through her so easily she had to break the kiss to breathe, gasping as her head fell to his shoulder, the gentle pulse of pleasure easing over her.

"Damn," he said roughly, sounding very unlike Dan and sexier than hell. He held her and she felt how hard he was and wanted to provide him some relief, too. Still, as the pleasure passed, awkwardness settled in. She couldn't quite meet his eyes, her voice soft.

"Do you…?" she asked, as her hand lowered to touch him.

"No, not now. Not here," he said, stopping her progress and tipping her face up so he could look at her. It was so unexpectedly intimate that she couldn't decide whether to escape or ask for more.

They stood like that, amazed and frozen in the moment for what seemed like a long, long time.

"Have dinner with me tonight, Jodie. Not Jason. Me," he said.

She was finding it hard to focus, her body still warm from coming, and her eyes wouldn't seem to move away from his mouth.

"I—I can't…I mean, I'll cancel with Jason, but with Ginger gone I think I have to stay and finish what I didn't get done today."

"Tomorrow night, then."

She couldn't say no, overwhelmed with the desire to be with him. The bell over the door rang and they jumped apart, and she saw Ginger and Jason walk in together.

Jodie tried to compose herself, but it was difficult after having Dan's kiss trip her trigger, and her body was still begging for more.

One look at Jason's stormy expression and she knew that he'd seen them together, or at least he knew something had happened, if not what. Ginger looked surprised, too, but her mouth quirked up in a part smile. "Sorry I'm late again, Jodie…or maybe not."

Jodie looked at her with wide eyes, and the two men stared, saying nothing. Jodie crossed the space, flipping the sign to Closed and locking the door. They were closing soon anyway.

"Jason, I'm sorry—"

"What? Sorry for crawling all over another guy when you're supposed to be with me?"

She arched an eyebrow, a chill of anger pushing away the heat of moments before. "I am not *with* you. We went out to dinner, and that was it. Even if it had been more, I wouldn't be with you. I'm not *with* anyone, ever, and I don't want to be."

Jason's attitude was harder, meaner and not at all like the shy science guy. An act?

He barked a laugh. "Oh, I *know* what you are, believe me. I was just hoping to get some action before you moved on to the next one in line." He glanced sideways at Dan. "Looks like you jumped in ahead of me."

Jodie watched as Dan moved quickly from the other side of the counter. She'd never seen him so angry.

"Watch yourself, Kravitz," he warned, standing at her side where the cologne washed over her again. Her hormones wouldn't settle down. She'd only had two cookies; they'd never had this strong an effect on her. They were supposed to affect the man—the man you were trying to attract or seduce.

Oh fudge. Maybe that's what had Dan so worked up and in Jason's face, acting so unlike himself.

"Jason, you need to leave. Needless to say, I won't be seeing you tonight or any night," she managed to say sternly.

She heard him mutter *whore* under his breath. Dan stepped forward, but she moved faster, swinging and slapping his skinny face so hard that it knocked his head back.

"Don't come in here. Ever," she said in a voice coated with ice.

"Don't worry about that," he said, holding a hand to his jaw and glaring at her and Dan.

"This isn't over, I promise," he said to Dan as Jodie held the door open.

"Oh, I really think it is," Dan said smugly, looking at her proudly.

His gaze was enough to make her nipples poke out again, begging for his attention, and she closed her eyes, turning away from him as she shut the door. Whatever was happening, Jodie knew she had a problem.

4

I'M NOT WITH ANYONE, and I don't want to be.

Jodie's words to Jason had haunted Dan all Monday and came back to him again as he got ready for dinner. She'd meant it; he knew her well enough for that. The problem was that in the second their lips had met, he'd wanted her to be with him. For good.

He'd gone to the shop with the clear purpose of kissing her, though he had simply hoped to change her mind about Jason. Having her discover for herself what an ass the guy was had been a bonus.

Examining himself in the mirror, he was assaulted by doubt that didn't feel the least bit masculine or comfortable. He'd been the way he was for so long, it was strange to look in the mirror and see someone else. Finding that he really wanted to impress Jodie, he'd skipped out of the lab early to meet his sister. The result was several new designer suits and casuals, a new haircut, new contact lenses.

"You look great—stop second-guessing yourself. You should have done this years ago," his sister Donna said, peeking around the corner. She was the older of the two of them, and had gently suggested many times he exchange his glasses for contacts and dress more stylishly.

Dan was used to being locked in a lab or valued for what was in his head, not on his body. Who cared what he wore?

Jodie never seemed to mind, he thought stubbornly, shifting in the stylish Ralph Lauren blazer and pants, even though they fit well. She certainly hadn't minded yesterday, but that wasn't a fair test, either.

"I suppose it's all right," he said reluctantly, pushing his hand through the short, spiky cut that he couldn't quite get used to. The stylist was right; he couldn't feel the gel she'd instructed him to use.

"You can afford to dress well, and you should. I always suspected my little brother was a chick magnet, and I was right," Donna declared, checking him out in the mirror in triumph.

He frowned. "I don't think you're objective enough to make that assessment."

"Believe me, dear brother, Jodie doesn't stand a chance."

Though with the cologne he was wearing—a recent experiment for a cosmetic company that had a similar pheromone extract for men as the Passionate Hearts cookies had for women—he knew it didn't matter.

He'd seen the dramatic effect when Jodie hadn't only been attracted, she'd been all over him. In fact, maybe the formulation had worked a little too well—Jodie had been driven to orgasm by a kiss.

He recalled how she'd broken their kiss on a sharp gasp, her eyes opening wide then slowly fluttering shut, her mouth forming the most beautiful bow as she'd let the pleasure take her over. Dan had never seen anything so erotic in his life, and he wanted to see it again, ideally with them both naked and with him deep inside of her. While Jodie had found some release, he hadn't, and his body was fully charged, on the edge.

He had scrubbed away the cologne in the shower, but he suspected something was off in his formula. Women had been reacting all day.

They watched him as he walked by, and stood closer than they should. He'd had to ask the saleslady who had brought him clothes to try on to leave the dressing room. It was interesting from an experimental perspective, if annoying from a personal one. Maybe his endocrine system was so cranked that it was making the cologne work overtime. It was hard to tell.

He definitely had to work out some kinks in his formulations, but for now, maybe the attractant would help smooth over any awkward moments from their unexpected kiss. While he was sure any of the women he'd met over the course of the day would have been open to helping him ease some of his sexual tension, there was only one woman he wanted. Unfortunately, he couldn't have her. Not yet, anyway.

He would simply control himself and not let anything else happen between them. If anything ever did happen again, it wouldn't be the result of the stimulus caused by cookies or the cologne.

"You've liked her for so long, Dan, but are you sure

this is smart?" Donna said, looking at him with worried eyes. She'd kept her counsel when it came to Jodie, but he knew his sister disapproved of his pal's playing the field.

"It's only dinner, Donna."

"Yeah, right. You've had dinner with her hundreds of times, and it never required a makeover."

He sighed. "It's just that…when I saw her with Jason, I wanted to punch his face in. I never had such a visceral reaction before. And when we kissed, well…I think now we should see if we're anything more than friends."

"And what if you're not? What if something does happen? Can you go back to being only that?"

It would be difficult, he knew, and paused before answering. Could he go back to watching the men drift in and out of Jodie's life, in and out of her bed?

"I don't know. Like Mom says, we'll cross that bridge when we come to it."

"Well, sometimes people fall off the bridge and get hurt."

"Maybe it's time for that, too. I've lived my life in a sort of bubble, Donna, as you've reminded me on so many occasions," he added, turning to her. "I love you for worrying about me, but I am thirty-three. I've never committed my heart fully to anything but my work. If I get hurt…well…we'll chalk this up to a failed experiment, I guess."

Donna shook her head. "I don't know, Dan. I like Jodie, she's a good friend, but I can't help thinking she doesn't deserve you. Not with the way she goes through men like shirts." She smiled fondly. "With this new look, your brains, and your bank account, you could have any woman you want now."

"That's the point, though. I want her. Always have. She goes through men like shirts because she doesn't think she deserves better."

"And you think you can show her otherwise? She's a grown woman, and she lives her life the way she wants to."

"I've got to try. Time to get in the game," he said, sounding far more confident than he felt. Losing Jodie from his life would be a serious blow, he knew. So he had to make sure that didn't happen.

JODIE WOKE UP Monday close to noon, having worked late with Ginger and then being unable to sleep as she worried about Dan. She lay in bed for a long time worrying about the memory of their kiss. On the upside, the entire episode had revealed Jason to be a complete jerk, but on the downside, she'd rubbed tongues and climaxed with her very best friend.

What had happened between them to make them combust like that? She buried her head farther down into the pillows. God, this was a mess. Dan was the one guy she could count on, the one man who accepted her as she was and didn't ask for more than her friendship. She hadn't known he was coming by the shop, but no doubt stuffing two Passionate Hearts down her gullet right before he walked in had been to blame.

It didn't explain her reaction, which she put down to sexual frustration and being caught off guard. Though if he'd caused that kind of seismic reaction in her body from a kiss and a simple touch, what would he be able to do if they—

No.

It had clearly been her fault, and she had to make it right.

Jumping out of bed, she showered and got dressed. She was meeting him later for dinner, but maybe she could find him at the lab where she could explain about the cookies and apologize. Then they could catch a movie and get back on their old footing.

Relieved at having a workable plan, she headed out to find him, certain that she could fix this and move on.

It only took a few minutes by train before she was at the university, finding her way deep into the belly of the science building where Dan's office and attached lab were located, but she couldn't find him anywhere.

"Hey, Sherry, is Dan around?" she asked the secretary down the hall who oversaw the suite of labs and offices.

"He took off early today," Sherry said with a smile. "I think he has a hot date or something. He might stop back, but I don't know for sure."

Jodie bit back a groan. Great. She didn't want to do this over the phone or at dinner.

"Do you mind if I leave him a note in the lab, just in case?"

"Nah, you're fine, help yourself."

Jodie smiled and scooted back to the lab where she formulated a note in her mind and searched for some blank paper on Dan's desk.

Though she wasn't snooping, her eye caught sight of her name, strangely, and she looked closer, curious.

Pushing other papers aside, she skipped over the array of formulas and symbols that made no sense to her and saw what seemed to be notes dated the day before—*about her.*

Unabashedly picking up the entire notebook, her eyes devoured the pages, her heart hammering as she skipped over the parts she didn't understand to absorb the parts she understood all too well.

Dan had used her. She'd been an experiment as he tested the formulations of a new cologne, as far as she could see, that worked similar to how the extract in her cookie frosting worked, only for men.

She remembered commenting on the cologne, and how the minute she'd laid eyes on him, she couldn't think straight. When he'd come closer, he'd become downright irresistible.

He hadn't told her, hadn't warned her, and her cheeks flamed anew as she read the notes written about her response—in rather graphic detail.

Anger and betrayal coursed through her. Her first instinct was to take the notes, burn them or stuff them down his throat and tell him, like Jason, never to darken her door again.

Then the hurt set in, and her eyes blurred with tears as she looked up at the clock. She rushed to the door of the lab, closing it as sobs choked her.

This was Dan. There must be an explanation, but she couldn't think of one—it had been pretty obvious. He came to the shop wearing something meant to stimulate women's sexual attraction to him, and he'd let her make a fool of herself without stopping her or warning her. According to the notes, it had all been on purpose. An experiment to see if the cologne worked.

Still, their friendship demanded she give him a chance to explain. Which she would—after she taught him a lesson he wouldn't soon forget. Hopefully their friendship could survive this, but maybe not.

No one duped her like this. No man took advantage of her that way without paying for it ten times over. Every memory of every time her father had enjoyed making her look stupid or foolish in front of others played through her mind, and she shoved the memories away. She was different now.

Leaving the lab, she made her way to the bakery and grabbed a stash of Passionate Hearts cookies, taking most of the tray as Ginger watched with interest, but Jodie didn't feel like talking about it.

She'd have to run an extra mile every day for a week to burn off the calories, but she was a woman with a plan, and extra calories were a sacrifice she'd have to make.

DAN WASN'T NERVOUS when he stood outside Jodie's apartment door, but he was anticipating what was going to happen. After the kiss in the bakery, it was difficult, impossible really, to treat this evening like any other. This was a big deal. This was Jodie.

He knocked, hoping the flowers he'd bought on the way over weren't too much. He'd seen the dark pink calla lilies, and for some reason they reminded him of

Jodie—the color of her lips—and he couldn't resist the romantic gesture.

When the door opened, he almost dropped them.

She wasn't dressed for dinner. She was dressed for sex.

"Hey," she said with a smile. "I thought we might stay in tonight. Order something from takeout."

He didn't have words to reply, his brain fried as he took in the sleek swath of scarlet satin that hung over her slim form from two thin spaghetti straps, one fallen loose over her arm.

She'd put her dark hair up in a haphazard fashion that begged someone to pull out the pin and let it loose.

"These are for you," he said, his eyes finding their way back up to meet hers after noting the way the satin clung to her hips and teased the tips of what could only be bare breasts underneath the material.

"They're pretty," she commented, though she didn't look anywhere but at him. "Come on in. If you still want to go out, I could put something on."

"No," he said, maybe a tad too quickly, pulling at his collar. He was overly warm, and he kept his eyes on her face so that he could try to control what was happening in his pants. She was so beautiful, wearing a slight bit of cosmetics that made her blue eyes smoky and her lips shine.

"You look incredible," he said.

She smiled, looking him over, appreciation shining in her eyes. "You, too. I don't think I've ever seen you dressed up before. You clean up good, Ellison. I like the new hair, too. How long have you worn contacts?"

He smiled. "It's Donna's influence. She's been nagging me for a long time to change my image, and I guess it was just…time."

For you, he added silently.

"She has great taste."

He laughed. "Yeah, she did a good job spending my money."

Jodie laughed, and he knew he'd heard her laugh a million times before, but this time it was like a touch, and his cock jerked in response.

He took off his jacket, warm and feeling overdressed, considering she was next to nude in that gown.

"So…what do you feel like?"

She quirked an eyebrow at him, her lips parting suggestively.

"I mean, for dinner. I can call in an order," Dan clarified.

His mouth was dry and in one gulp he downed the glass of wine she gave him. Now that she was closer, he saw the pink tint in her skin, the telltale flush around her throat and the darkening of her eyes that only meant one thing—the cologne's effect had not yet diminished.

"I'm not too hungry just yet. Maybe…later."

His eyebrows shot up. "Later?"

"Mmm-hmm." She smiled, stepping up close. "You know. After."

Her scent overcame him and he was now fully hard, his heart slamming in his chest. His brain was at the mercy of his body. He knew he was supposed to be resisting, taking control and making sure nothing happened, since it was simply the cologne she was responding to.

He'd forgotten about the strength of his own needs, his own response to her. That was harder to control, seemingly impossible at the moment, though he tried.

"That's not what I came here for, Jodie. I wanted to have dinner with you, and…"

"And?" she asked, leaning in to brush her lips over his.

Hot damn.

"I don't know. There's something we should do, or talk about, or something, but I can't seem to remember," he said roughly. Feeling like an actor from an old movie, he pulled her up close to him and crushed his mouth to hers in a kiss that let loose all the pent-up feelings, fantasies and desires he'd kept tightly contained for so long.

"You feel so good," he muttered against her mouth, his mind a haze of lust, his body leading the way. Sliding his hands over the silky slope of her back, he closed his palms gently over the curves of her backside and pressed her in against him, swallowing her gasp in another kiss.

He could feel the points of her breasts poking into his shirt. He broke the kiss to bend and suck one delicate nub through the material, rewarded as she shuddered, her hands digging into his shoulders.

"Dan," she breathed, then moaned, as he sucked a little harder.

Down on his knees now, he brought his hands to her delicate ankles, looking up at her.

"You're perfect, you know that?"

She shook her head and tried to step away, but he wouldn't let her. Only need drove him now, and the sole purpose of making sure she experienced every nuance of pleasure he could offer her.

His thumbs caressed the arches of her bare feet, his hands sliding slowly up her beautiful legs, over rounded calves, strong from her daily runs, lifting the dress as he went. He stopped to notice her knees in particular, planting a kiss on each as his fingers caressed the sensitive skin at the back.

"Most people think the knee is a simple hinge, but it's so amazingly complex…it bears so much weight, does so much work…and yours are absolutely perfect," he said. "There's the patella," he said, running his tongue over a small spot at the front. "And the articular surface," he whispered, kissing her on the inner side.

"Dan," she said, breathless, and he felt her shudder again as his fingers caressed the back—she liked that.

"Back here, under my fingers, the ligaments and muscles that all work together when you move. You move very gracefully, Jodie," he said, his hands riding up a little higher. "I don't think I ever told you that."

"Why would you?"

"Because even as your friend, I couldn't ignore how lovely you are," he said honestly, pushing the bottom of the dress up to reveal shapely thighs and finally, the mystery of what hid beneath the satin.

He held the material bunched in one fist against her hip, moving his other hand over the almost bare skin of her abdomen. Swallowing hard, he leaned in to plant a kiss just above the softly swollen lips of her sex, her flowery scent encompassing him.

"Dan!" she said, her cry mingling need and surprise, maybe confusion. He looked up, though it was difficult to break away.

"You want me to stop?"

She looked at him for a long moment with dark, blazing azure eyes and shook her head.

"No. Please don't stop."

It wasn't supposed to go this way, Jodie thought, looking down at Dan kneeling before her, so incredibly sexy. The new hair, his transformed image almost made him a stranger, but as their eyes met, she knew an intimate familiarity.

She knew his face better than anyone else's. She knew him happy, sad, intense, frustrated and angry—but she'd never seen him like this. His jaw was strong, his lips sensual and full—how had she never noticed before? His hands...his long, nimble fingers...were magic.

She hadn't counted on this.

Consuming enough Passionate Hearts to inflame a navy battalion, Jodie had planned to take him to the brink, arouse him until he couldn't think straight and then show him the door. In all the ways she'd envisioned the scenario, she'd stayed in cool control, demanding an explanation for his betrayal.

Now, she just wanted his mouth on her, as soon and as completely as possible.

She knew it was the cologne—and in this case, his

cologne mixed with a whopping dose of Passionate Hearts frosting extract—but she didn't care.

The way he looked at her, so deeply, so sincerely, she could almost believe this was real. When he slipped gentle fingers between the slick folds of her labia, she stopping worrying about it.

She wanted him to have both hands free and lifted her gown, pulling the entire thing up over her head and throwing it over a chair, standing naked before him.

His eyes deepened to a rich espresso, taking in every inch of her so acutely that she shivered, but he didn't say a word. He didn't need to—his fingers were doing the talking, stroking her lightly, playing and exploring as he inspected her with an intense gaze that missed nothing.

She trembled, heat spreading from the touch of his fingers outward, her muscles tightening as the touch triggered her nerve endings into a response. She reached out to stabilize herself by grabbing the back of the sofa, holding herself in check as she could.

This time she wouldn't be alone, making herself vulnerable and exposed when she lost control. She'd make sure she took him with her.

"Ah, I think one of us has too many clothes on," she said, trying to catch her breath.

"I enjoy this. You came for me in the shop, when we kissed. It was amazing. I want to make it happen again."

She smiled. "Me, too, believe me. But not alone. I want you with me."

"You think you can hold back?" he said in playful

challenge, finding the pearl of her clit with his thumb, expertly parting her flesh and then diving in to plant a wet, hot kiss on the spot.

Who was this incredible, playful and daring stranger? Certainly not her Dan...

She moaned, her legs trembling with the effort to resist bearing down and taking what he was offering as his tongue teased her. How had he gotten so good at this, having dated so few women?

Dan obviously had secrets, not that she was complaining. Whether it was the frosting, the cologne or the man, she knew she'd never gotten this hot this fast with anyone, ever.

"You're beautiful, Jodie," he whispered, bending so that he could flick his tongue up against her, sending her skyrocketing. Her body tensed and she hissed out a breath through her teeth, trying to hold on.

When he removed his hands to shift position, she sighed in relief and dropped to her knees, face-to-face with him.

Her best friend. Her lover. At least for tonight.

"Both of us, Dan," she insisted, reaching for the clasp of his belt but letting her hand drift down to cradle his erection in her palm first, feeling through his pants that he was more than enough for her. "Please," she said, meeting his eyes and squeezing.

His jaw went slightly slack as she massaged him and she regained her sense of power, grabbed back some control. But not for long.

Within minutes, they were both naked and she subjected him to the same slow inspection he'd offered her, stopping at strategic spots to touch and taste, and by the time he gently pushed her down on the soft living room carpet, she was sure she'd lose her mind if he didn't get inside of her.

But Dan was a scientist. He was methodical and patient. He experimented, starting with a gentle bite by her ankle, working his way upward, as if trying to find the tiniest spot that would drive her crazy,

He observed, sitting back to watch as he played with her breasts, tweaking her nipples as she arched her back in a desperate attempt to get closer, to find what she craved.

Control? What control? Dan was the one in control, she realized with a shiver by the time he finally grabbed a condom from his wallet. Poised between her thighs, the broad crown of his cock slightly nudging her as he stroked himself, he still didn't rush.

"Dan," Jodie practically panted. She never begged, but she needed him more than she needed to be in control. "Please…"

She gasped as he finally leaned over her, stealing her moan with a deep kiss as he slid into her body in one firm thrust, hands planted on either side of her shoulders. As he started moving, the rhythm robbed her of all remaining questions.

5

DAN DIDN'T USUALLY DREAM, or if he did, he was one of those people who didn't remember any of the details.

Waking up naked in bed with Jodie, her face on his chest, her leg thrown over him, he was sure that he was dreaming, though he could remember *every* detail.

His morning meditation routine, normally the first thing he did upon waking, was the last thing from his mind. Jodie's soft, silky hair was splayed over him, and his immediate response to her closeness was the predictable male one. Meditating was not what he wanted to do right now.

Sliding gently out from beneath her, he smiled as she mumbled grumpily in her sleep. Jodie slept like the dead. But he was going to run a couple more experiments, seeing just what would make her wake up.

Facedown on the mattress now, her arms up over her head, he let his eyes wander over her delectable bare curves as she stretched out before him like a feast.

She was incredible. More so than he ever imagined.

He reached over, running his hands lightly across her

back, massaging gently. Her skin was warm satin, and his cock was hard and eager, but he had only patience when it came to Jodie. He'd waited for this forever, and now he was going to take his time.

She sighed in her sleep, obviously liking his touch, and he kept at it, working his way lower, curving his hands over her beautiful bottom and raining kisses along the way.

Still, she slept.

Kneeling in between her already parted thighs, he slid his hand down between her legs, petting the perfectly trimmed pubic hair that covered her flesh, feeling his fingers moisten as he found the hard nub of her clit and rubbed, eliciting a sleepy moan and then a gasp.

When she lifted her bottom, sleepily asking for more, Dan found his patience was running out and, ever so slowly, he entered her, slowly and easily filling the warm channel of her body as he lay down over her, stretching out, winding his fingers into hers. They'd used condoms for the first few times last night, but then mutual disclosure had revealed the barrier unnecessary.

He moved languorously, and she responded by rotating her hips in a delicious, seductive swirl. She was with him, he knew, even though her eyes remained closed.

Her breathing deepened, her cheeks turning pink as their movements became faster, more insistent, and he knew she was close. After just one night together, he'd studied and memorized the signals of her body. He knew what she liked. He wanted to know more.

He pushed himself back to his knees, grabbing her hips and pumping hard to find his own release, pouring himself into her as she cried out, her pretty red nails clawing into the sheets.

"Oh, Dan, that was so good," she said, her eyes still closed.

"It's always good with you, Jodie," he said, the warmth that stole over him having nothing to do with sex. He'd had plenty of sexual encounters—more than Jodie probably thought—but he had never experienced anything like this. Dreaming of being with Jodie was nothing like the real thing. He was glad she felt the same way.

He chuckled when she snored lightly two seconds later. He dropped back down beside her, watching her sleep. She was his, but he knew the very idea of that wouldn't wash with her. Jodie wouldn't give in that easily, not even with him.

Even though she would tell him he was crazy, that she was a strong woman in charge of her own life and that her past was behind her—and that would be true—he also knew better than anyone that childhood wounds had left her believing she wasn't worth loving. He knew she would bolt from any emotional entanglement past friendship. He knew he had to convince her differently.

So while she dozed, he planned.

JODIE SAT on the edge of the bed, listening to Dan in the shower. She'd dozed after their sleepy sex, which she'd thought at first was just a hot dream, though it certainly felt better than any sex dream she'd ever had before. Now she was awake. She'd waited Dan out, or so she thought, until he finally got out of bed and went in to use the shower.

She should have known better than to think she could fool him. Chuckling, he'd leaned over and whispered in her ear that he knew she was really awake, betrayed by subtle changes in her breathing and eye movements, but that she could join him in the shower if she wanted.

And the hard part was, that she wanted him again, and again, even though they'd nearly spent each other completely the night before. Her body was craving more Dan, but her mind was reeling.

What had she done? This was a mess.

She stood and started to pace, still naked, thinking back to the night before. It hadn't just been the cookies, though her massive consumption of icing had probably helped things along. Dan had to have been wearing his cologne, even though she hadn't detected the scent. But it was clear he had planned this, planned to get her into bed, planned to seduce her as part of his experiment.

She'd known that, and she thought she could resist. Maybe she could have, but whatever he put in the formula he was wearing was potent stuff. Like the man himself. She still couldn't get over his stamina, and his creativity.

A little voice in the back of her head *tsk-tsked*—could she really blame all of this on him?

Yes. It was easier to be angry and unfair than to think about any one of the emotions rolling around inside of her at the moment. She loved Dan—as a friend.

She didn't want love otherwise, which was why she kept her sex life active but separate from her emotional ties. She and Dan had gone and messed that up now, and it would probably cost them their friendship, she accepted, her heart breaking.

Well, he'd gotten what he wanted—and plenty of it—so now they both had some hard choices to make. Grabbing her robe as the shower stopped, she tied it around her middle, holding on to her anger like a shield as he walked out with only a towel around his trim waist.

Oh hell, she thought, her nipples hardening.

"Morning, hon," he said, walking over to grab his briefs and pants, pulling them on and getting dressed as if their world wasn't now ass over teakettle. "You want to go down to the Waffle House? I'm starved," he said, sliding a sexy grin in her direction.

Hon? Waffles? Jodie's thoughts echoed. "You want waffles?" she asked, incredulous as he crossed over, planted a light kiss on her lips and ruffled her hair.

"Yeah, sounds good. You know, on average, people our size and weight will burn around one-hundred-fifty calories per hour during the typical sexual encounter. I figure after what we did last night, which was far from typical, and how many times we did it, we definitely can indulge in waffles. Maybe bacon," he said with wicked enthusiasm.

Jodie didn't move. How could he stand here and act as if everything was normal, as if they hadn't just pulled the very foundations of over a decade of friendship from the roots?

It was hard to believe what she was hearing, and yet again, maybe not. This was Dan. He was able to compartmentalize his life even more so than she could. For him, everything had a rational explanation.

She wasn't sure what made her angrier—that he'd used chemically enhanced cologne to seduce her, or that he could be so casual about banging her brains out all night, or that she was so upset about it. She was supposed to be the one who walked away, who was casual in the morning.

"You can get whatever breakfast you want," she said coolly. "Apparently you're very good at getting what you want. By any means necessary," she added, unable to keep the hurt from her voice.

"What do you mean, Jodie?" he asked, but he wasn't sounding casual now, just a bit confused.

"You know *exactly* what I am talking about!" Jodie said between her teeth, trying to force back tears and hating how her emotions were taking over. "You used that cologne, your new special formula, to seduce me! I was an *experiment*," she said, her voice breaking as she turned her back on him, gulping down the sob that threatened to escape.

Jodie would not give any man the satisfaction of seeing her cry. Her father was the last man who'd done that—but that was when she was nine, and she'd never let it happen again. Dan touched her shoulder and she yanked away.

"Jodie, please," he said, and she put up her hand, turning her head away from him.

"No. I don't even want to hear it. I thought we were more to each other than that. I always thought you were…different," she said, suddenly exhausted again.

"But you're not. So I hope you enjoyed it, and you can just leave now, okay? Just go get your breakfast," she said, walking to the bathroom and into the shower.

She didn't want to see him go, she realized, and sank under the hot water, having a good cry, all by herself.

When she came back out, feeling like crap but intent on starting her day, she pulled on some clothes and thought about breakfast. She was so hungry she could smell food, no doubt from her neighbors. Apparently Dan was right about one thing—she probably had burned all of the calories from the cookies she'd consumed in their hours of crazy sex.

She walked into the kitchen, expecting to be alone, and found Dan there, sitting at the table with coffee he'd apparently made.

She didn't know Dan could make coffee.

He was reading a paper, and looked up, meeting her gaze steadily. "I made some breakfast. Sit down, get some food, and let's talk this out," he said matter-of-factly.

She didn't know he could cook, either. She'd always brought food to him, and assumed he ate out the rest of the time. She hadn't known he'd be dynamite in bed—or how far he was willing to go to get her there.

"Well, aren't you just full of surprises," she said stiffly, moving over to the stove.

The eggs staying warm in the pan smelled spicy and made her mouth water, so though she wanted to tell him to stick his eggs where the sun didn't shine, she crossed the room and filled her plate, grabbing some toast from a plate on the stove, as well. Coffee was already poured for her by the time she sat, and she ate without saying one more word to him.

He didn't seem to mind. He was reading something that appeared to have gained his full attention, and after she finished her breakfast, refilled her coffee and noisily put her dishes—and his—in the sink, she started to wonder if he knew she was there at all.

How was he able to set her off balance so easily?

"Dan? Are you going to sit in the middle of my home reading all day? I have things to do."

"Like what? I thought today was your day off?"

"Like…like…I do things on my day off. Personal things."

"Errands?"

She actually had no errands to run, but wasn't going to admit that. "Yes."

"I can go with you. We can talk."

Jodie closed her eyes, defeated. "Why are you doing this?"

"Doing what? Making you breakfast? Wanting to talk?"

"No…yes. I mean, there's nothing to talk about. What happened happened. And we both know why it happened."

"It happened because we've been attracted to each other for some time, and it was bound to happen sooner or later."

"I don't think—"

"It's true. I could prove it mathematically if you like, the odds of two people as close as we are, over a number of years—"

"Stop, please. No math," she begged. "Don't you think your little experiment with the cologne would throw off your results, anyway? This was attraction that you manufactured, and you know it."

Dan was nonplussed. "I didn't wear the cologne last night, Jodie. I admit I did wear it to the shop, yes, but I didn't wear it last night, though there was some residual effect. I could see it with women's responses to me all day."

"Like what?"

He shrugged. "They wanted to stand closer, their pupils dilated, their bodies and postures showed clear evidence of attraction. So I knew the cologne was probably still active in some way, even though I had tried to shower it off. For that reason, I had promised not to let anything happen with us last night, but when I saw you...it was like..." He caught her gaze and held it, his own so intense it was like a touch. "It was like an explosion."

He frowned then and kept talking. "But let's back up here a minute. I admit, the cologne could have had some effect, but you were clearly intent on seduction last night. The clothes, the invitation...and you planned that before I showed up at the door. Long before the cologne would have been an issue."

He stared at her, not saying another word, and she swallowed hard.

Nailed. In more ways than one.

Throwing her hands up, she knew there was no point in denying it. "Okay, fine, that's true. I had planned to get back at you for using me with that cologne, for that kiss. I thought I'd give you a dose of your own medicine and lead you on a little, and then let you know I knew it was the cologne, and leave you…" She stopped, feeling her face heat as she realized what she was admitting.

Dan finished her thought for her. "You figured you'd get me all hot and bring me to the edge, and then leave me there? And let me know why?"

She let out the breath she was holding. "Yes."

"I see. I guess there's one other thing I'm still confused about."

"What's that?"

Dan stood and walked over, standing close to her, though he didn't try to touch her. "I am attracted to you, Jodie. I've wanted you for years, and it's been hell watching you with other men. I won't deny I wanted you last night, but I didn't intend to sleep with you—until I saw you. And I think my reaction felt…enhanced, as well. Like maybe you were helping things along as well? And I don't just mean with that sexy nightie and the seductive talk."

Jodie looked away. "I might have had a few cookies, just to teach you a lesson. To show you what it felt like."

"I figured. So the effects of the cookies and the remnant of the cologne in my bloodstream…do you think that's all we can attribute our behavior to?"

Why was her heart pounding so hard in her chest? She wanted to take a step back, but the wall was right behind her.

"What do you mean? Of course that's what happened. It was a bad plan in the first place, and I never considered that I wouldn't be able to resist the effects of the cologne," she said, her voice softer than she wished.

"Your pulse has spiked, your cheeks are flushed, and your pupils are dilated," he said, raising a hand to her cheek.

"It's that stupid cologne. Does it ever wear off?"

Dan smiled. "There's no way the cologne is still having any major effect at this point. The ingredients break down over forty-eight hours. So what else do you think could be causing this reaction?"

"I'm furious with you, that's what," she said. "I want you to leave."

"I think you want me to leave because you know your response isn't having anything to do with the cologne," he said softly. "Neither is mine. Whatever is happening right here, right now, it's just us, Jodie."

She did step back, sure that some distance would give her sanity, but he stepped forward, trapping her against the wall. Hardness pressed against the softness of her stomach, and she couldn't stop the rush of heat between her legs.

"Dan, we can't do this," she said, sounding more desperate than she wished.

"Why not? It appears we have fantastic chemistry, with or without additives," he said with a brief kiss to the edge of her lips. "Though I am always interested in experimenting, I've never had much use for…implements…toys. But maybe we could explore…"

Jodie's mind entered total meltdown mode as she even considered the idea. Dan tying her to the rails of her bed and experimenting with her vibrator…or maybe she'd tie him and experiment with warm honey….

"Stop," she said sharply, though she was speaking to the direction of her own thoughts more than she was to him. Still, Dan nodded shortly and stepped back. She appreciated it, and also regretted losing the closeness.

He had her so confused she didn't know what she wanted.

"Jodie, can I suggest something?"

"As long as it doesn't have to do with sex toys, yes," she said.

"I want to apologize for the cologne. I did use it the day in the shop, because I had an agenda, as well. I needed to stop you from seeing Jason. He's a…he's an ass. I've wanted you for so long, and I couldn't stand the idea of you with him. So I…I gambled."

Shocked by his confession and his honesty, Jodie relaxed slightly. "You were jealous of Jason?"

Dan looked minutely uncomfortable, but nodded. "I'm jealous of all of them, jealous of anyone who touches you, of who gets to be with you. But the rest were strangers. With Jason…I could…it was just too much."

Now, when she thought he couldn't rock her world any more than he already had, he went and tilted it entirely in the other direction.

It was a revelation of sorts. She'd never had any idea that Dan could be jealous. She'd always just thought of him as her friend. As a friend, she supposed she could meet him halfway, all things considered.

"I'm sorry, too. For the cookies, and for planning to

seduce you, and leave you high and dry. We've been friends too long. I should have just come and talked to you," she said, truly regretful now that she had calmed down.

"Thank you."

She blew out a sigh. "So I guess we just try to put this behind us? To pretend this never happened, to save our friendship?" she said, walking to the other side of the kitchen to get some distance.

Could she? Could she really forget last night?

"I guess I wasn't clear," Dan said, smiling ruefully. "You make things topsy-turvy. I look at you, and it's hard to think straight."

Her breath caught. Lots of men had said things to her like that, but none of them with the depth of emotion that Dan had. The way he was looking at her led her to believe he wasn't interested in going back to being friends at all.

Uh-oh.

"What I meant to say," he continued, "was that not only would it be impossible for us to forget what happened last night, but we *shouldn't* forget it. How can we ever be with each other again without wanting more?"

Her heart sank. He was right.

"So I guess we have to keep our distance? Let things cool down, and over time, maybe we can make it work, if we try?" she suggested, her throat constricting at the idea of losing Dan at all, even short-term. She hated feeling so needy, but couldn't seem to help it. It was *Dan*.

He closed the space between them, taking her in his

arms and holding her close. "No, Jodie. What I mean is that we should do the exact opposite. We should be lovers. Exclusive lovers. Just you and me."

DAN WATCHED THE COLOR drain from Jodie's face and grabbed her shoulders, helping her to one of the kitchen chairs.

"Hey, are you okay?"

He hadn't expected such a drastic reaction to his proposition. Maybe laughter or something along the lines of her telling him he was completely crazy, or another angry flare of temper, but he hadn't expected her to look as though she would pass out.

"I'm fine," she said, wiping a hand over her face. "I don't…I think I misunderstood you."

"You heard me exactly right. We should be together, Jodie. It's…logical."

Her eyes widened. "How is any of this logical?"

He started to pace back and forth, the way he always did when he was formulating an idea.

"Well, we've already been in a committed relationship for over a decade," he posited, and when she tried to interrupt, he stopped her. "Just listen. Statistically our friendship has lasted longer than sixty-five percent of new marriages, which tend to dissolve within eight years," he said.

"But we aren't—"

"True, we aren't married, but we have spent a lot of time together. We've seen each other at our best and worst, and we've always communicated extremely well. We're there for each other, no matter what. On top of that, we've been successful business partners. That's even more impressive than beating the divorce statistics. Did you know that two out of three business partnerships fail within five years?"

She shook her head. "No I didn't but—"

"Additionally, you can't argue that our sexual compatibility is off the charts. Do you know the odds against the number of orgasms that you had—"

Jodie put up a hand. "No, I don't, and I don't think I want to. Listen, Dan, people can't become lovers based on statistics."

"Why not?"

She looked at him long and hard, as if trying to figure out whether he was serious.

"Well, because...they just don't."

"And maybe that's why they fail. You and I have history, we have background, we have *friendship*...now we have more. It's logical that our friendship would have developed into more over time. It's probably why neither of us has been permanently attracted to anyone else."

"That's a stretch."

"Maybe. But I hypothesize that we could be extremely happy and successful in a romantic relationship. We owe it to ourselves to try."

"You're forgetting a pretty big consideration, Dan."

"What?"

"I don't *want* a romantic relationship. I've lived my life without it, and no matter how many statistics you quote, I don't want this," she said quietly. "And you know me better than anyone. You know that's true."

Dan felt the words as a punch to the gut, but he

straightened, figuring that if she wouldn't be convinced in one way, maybe he could convince her in another.

"You haven't wanted it before, with anyone else, and I understand why. I know how you were hurt, Jodie, and I know—"

"You don't know everything, even if you think you do."

"I know enough. I also know you're cutting love out of your life, and if you do that, it's letting him win. Did you ever consider that? That living your life without love means he changed you forever? That you let him keep you from being happy in your life?"

She was so still Dan didn't know what to think. They stood like that for several long minutes, no one saying anything. Had he gone too far?

"I guess that's true," she said, surprising him, but still not looking at him. "I never thought about it like that."

"And?"

"I don't know. I am who I am, you know? I don't believe in love."

"Maybe I can help you change that. People change their beliefs all the time. It's the foundation of scientific thought, really, when you think about it."

"Who am I to thwart the very foundations of scientific reason?" she said, and Dan had to smile. He knew he was wearing her down.

"Exactly."

"I guess if I was ever going to risk any kind of permanent relationship, you would be the right choice? The logical choice?" She laughed, pushing a hand through her hair. "I can't believe I'm actually buying into this."

"It will work, Jodie. You'll see."

"Listen, Dan, I know you mean well, but—"

"No buts. Let's try this, Jodie. What do you have to lose? The sex between us is great, and we're friends. Why not give it a shot?" he asked. "We can see if it works, and if it doesn't, we'll leave it behind, and just go back to being friends?"

Dan was building an escape hatch, and he was okay with that, since he had no intention of letting her use it. He knew they could never go back to being simply friends. Ever.

So this experiment had to work.

She stared at him intently, shaking her head, and he felt his heart take a dive, sure he had lost his chance to convince her.

"Okay then," she said, dusting her hands on the side of her jeans. "You win. We can be friends with benefits for a while, but either of us can call time, and we just become friends again, right?"

"Yeah," Dan said with a smile. He'd won. Jodie was his. He'd make sure this worked.

And he was going to start right now, he thought, crossing the kitchen and catching her up close for a deep kiss, old-movie style, dipping her down low. She laughed at first, but before long, they were on their way to the kitchen tile, breathless.

Until they were interrupted by the shrill ring of her cordless phone on the wall.

"Don't answer, they'll leave a message," he said against her neck.

She was inclined to agree, as he had her both hot and bothered, but they froze as they heard Ginger's panicked voice. Jodie jumped up and grabbed the phone, tugging her clothes back into place.

Dan watched her face clear, red patches staining her cheeks—anger. She pushed a hand through her bangs.

"Okay, I'm sorry, Ginger, I'll be right there." She hung up and walked past him, grabbing his hand. "C'mon, we have to go."

"Where?"

"It's the shop. Someone broke in and wrecked the place."

6

"I CAN'T BELIEVE THIS," Jodie said in amazement, noting the destruction of the cases, the ruined baked goods on the floor, crushed.

Jason, she thought immediately.

He'd said she hadn't seen the last of him, but would a respected scientist really break into a business like a common thug? There had to be another explanation.

"We'll be closed for two days, at least," Ginger said dispiritedly. "The back is even worse. The orders were thrown and ripped, bags of flour and other ingredients dumped."

"Insurance will cover the damage, but not the lost business," Jodie said with a sigh, contemplating the slurs written in red spray paint across the glass display. It was clear disapproval of the sexy cookies she sold.

Dan hadn't said a word, but had been out back while she and Ginger had surveyed the damage up front and talked with police. Jody hadn't mentioned suspecting Jason, and tried to think through all the possibilities. There was no way the break-in was random.

"Hey, did you ever call that guy who stopped by and wanted to hook up with you?"

"No. He came in again, though, and I had to tell him no, in no uncertain terms. I can't expose Anna to this right now. She has enough to deal with without me dating."

Jodie nodded, patting Ginger's shoulder. She wasn't a mother, so she had no idea, and didn't want to say more than she had.

"Do you think that could have ticked him off?"

Ginger's eyes widened, but then she shook her head. "He didn't even get upset. He just said if I ever changed my mind, to call, and that he'd still stop by if that was okay, to see me here. I didn't want to encourage him, so I told him...oh crap. I told him customers are always welcome."

"Ouch. That was a bit cold."

Ginger's back stiffened. "I didn't want to encourage him."

"I know, I know. I'm sorry. I guess I'm trying to think of who else would do this, and your new admirer is the only other one I thought of. He doesn't seem the type, but you never can tell."

"Other one? Who else are you thinking about?"

"Jason—he was pretty pissed the other day. I just find it hard to think a guy of his stature would do something this...low."

"Then again, he might be smart enough to know that no one would suspect him, maybe."

Jodie nodded. She hadn't thought of it like that.

The police were done, and filed out the door. Now all

that was left was cleaning up the mess. Jodie closed the door as best she could behind them. A new lock would be installed before the end of the day, and she turned to hug Ginger tight.

"I think your idea about Jason could be right," Dan said from the doorway, joining their conversation.

Jodie turned, a slight riff of some new emotion wafting through her as she made eye contact with him, even in the middle of this mess.

"Dan, I know you don't like him, and I don't, either, but would he really stoop to something like this? Why?"

"There's only one good reason, especially since there was no money in the register and the safe is intact."

Awareness dawned painfully. "He came after the icing recipe."

"I'm afraid so."

She looked around and rushed to the back refrigerators. "All of the premixed icing I had made is gone, as well. None of the canisters are here. They're all gone."

"He'd need that to run tests, to back up the formula," Dan said.

"But isn't it patented or something? What can he do?" Ginger asked.

"He could share it on the Internet or do any number of things to ruin our sales. People wouldn't be able to get hold of the ingredients, but commercial manufacturers could, and then they just tweak something, call it something different, and there you have it," Dan said, wiping flour from the front of the designer shirt he'd been wearing all morning—the same one he'd come to her apartment in the night before.

"Or he could sell it, or who knows what else. But why wreck the rest of the place?" Ginger asked.

"To make it look like thugs did it. We can't prove he stole it. We can't prove it's him, unless we can catch him with the icing, but Jason is too clever to allow that to happen. But I know it in my gut," Dan said angrily. "And he's going to pay, one way or the other."

There it was again, Jodie thought, that little riff of excitement as she watched Dan's jaw square and his eyes darken. Kind of like when he was having an orgasm....

I am a sick, sick woman getting turned on in the middle of this chaos, she thought with a sigh. But now that the barn door was open, so to speak, on her and Dan having a friends-with-benefits relationship, she wanted him even more than she had before. And she was only now willing to be really honest with herself about how long she had been fantasizing about sleeping with Dan.

And she was happy a million times over that she hadn't done the deed with Jason Kravitz. What a monumental mistake that would have been. Jason had obviously been a stand-in for Dan, anyway, and the original was always better than a facsimile, she mused, and then turned her attention to the problem at hand.

"We can't know for sure who it was, unless the cops turn up a usable print, or some other kind of evidence," she said. "But Jason has an ego the size of King Kong. He's going to want us to know he did it, and he'll enjoy the fact that we can't do a thing about it without any evidence. He'd get such joy out of thinking he'd outsmarted us."

Dan met her eyes over the top of the case and nodded.

"Well, he's in for a surprise, then. When he makes his next move, we'll figure out how to beat him at his own game."

"And until then, we have massive cleaning and baking to do," Ginger said with a sigh. "I'll call Mom and see if Anna can stay overnight."

Jodie nodded, waving Dan off. "You don't have to stay, Dan. I know you probably have more important stuff to do."

He looked surprised. "Nothing is more important than being here with you right now. I want to help," he said plainly, his eyes and tone speaking volumes. Jodie couldn't help but be touched.

Ginger cleared her throat awkwardly. "Okay then. I think I'll start working out back so that we can get some baking done as soon as possible. Not that things aren't already pretty warm around here," she added with a chuckle as she left them alone.

Jodie and Dan smiled at each other. They'd figure it out, she knew. Together, like they always had.

TWO DAYS LATER THEY were open for business while a contractor finished replacing some of the casing glass that had been wrecked by their intruder. Life was almost normal again. There had been no word from Jason, and Dan had said he wasn't around the offices at all. They could simply speculate he was holed up somewhere, trying to decipher the frosting formula.

Every time Jodie thought of it, she wanted to strangle Jason Kravitz. But as time passed, she wondered if they didn't have it wrong? Maybe it was a random break-in? Her cookies were well advertised. Maybe it wasn't Jason. More likely some puritanical freak who didn't approve of her Passionate Hearts cookies or their side effects had finally decided to cause her some trouble.

They did live in a large city, and there was crime. Dan was still sure Jason was to blame, but Jodie wondered if that wasn't just a reaction to the fact that she and Jason had almost hooked up.

That was now in the past. They were exhausted but couldn't seem to keep their hands off each other. She'd almost been late for work again this morning, and Dan for a meeting, as well.

"So, you and Dan are an item now, huh?" Ginger inquired casually, though with a sparkle in her eye. "I always thought you two had some chemistry between you. And it's nice that you're friends. Friendship is a great thing to build a future on," she added, wiping down the counter as Jodie finished boxing up an order for delivery.

"Future? Don't go there, my friend. Dan and I have agreed we're just friends, and that's all we'll ever be. Friends with benefits maybe, but that's all. So you can keep that romantic imagination of yours in check."

"Really, Jodie? I thought you were the expert on men. Don't you see how he looks at you?" Ginger stopped working, obviously surprised. "The man is besotted.

And for what it's worth, you look at him exactly the same way."

Jodie pushed down irritation, or was it another emotion altogether? Fear? Apprehension?

"You have it wrong, Ginger. Believe me, Dan and I do care about each other. We have for years, and so we already have a relationship. We're giving in to this fantasy, this chemistry, but it will wear off. Trust me, it always does."

"Sure, after you've been married for years. And then it turns into something better."

"There's no need to get nasty and start using the *M* word," Jodie said with a frown.

The conversation was abbreviated when the bell over the door rang. The laughter and goofing around stopped when Jodie saw the man walk in and Ginger's color fading.

"Ginger, are you okay?" Jodie asked quietly as the man hovered by the door for a moment, then advanced.

"Hi, Scott. What are you doing here?" she said, both in response to Jodie's question, and to the man who now stood uncomfortably before the counter. Jodie went to her side, straightening her spine and set her hands on her hips, eying Ginger's ex.

So this was Scott. Tall, lanky, raven-haired with a pale complexion and poetic features that were too soft for Jodie's liking. His little girl looked just like him. What a difficult reminder for Ginger, Jodie realized.

How did she do it? Jodie had completely repressed that she had her own father's eyes, his coloring. She couldn't look in the mirror every day if she thought that.

Jodie's impulse to protect her friend was fierce, coming from some unknown emotional well, certainly from her past with her father.

"I need to talk to you, Ginger, and since you haven't answered my calls the last few days, I had no choice but to try to catch you here," he said.

"I've been busy," Ginger said tightly.

"If you're not here as a customer, you should probably leave," Jodie said. She eyed the man coolly but felt Ginger's hand on her arm.

"I can deal with it, Jodie. Do you mind if I take ten minutes?"

"Take as long as you need," Jodie said, nodding. "I'll be right out back."

"I won't be long, but thanks," Ginger said with a tense smile.

Jodie made herself scarce, but barely, hovering by the corner of the kitchen since there were no customers out front to give her an excuse to be at the counter, where it was easier to eavesdrop.

As it was, she couldn't hear anything and her thoughts wandered back over their conversation about Dan. Were they getting into something too deep? Was she fooling herself?

She and Dan, for as long as they'd been friends, moved in completely different circles. If it hadn't been for college, their paths never would have crossed.

Jodie wondered how well their lifestyles would mesh now and an idea formed in the back of her mind, but she was distracted by the ring of the bell again as Scott left.

Ginger stood planted in place, looking shell-shocked, her hand at her lips. Jodie couldn't stand it and walked out.

"What did he want? Are you okay?"

"Yeah, I'm okay, I guess," she said vaguely, walking back to where Jodie was, picking up a white towel, but just standing still and looking out the door where her ex had just left.

"Ginger, what is it?"

"He…he wants to get back together. To try again."

"Are you kidding me?"

"That's what I said. I figure he's just going through another one of his stages. Maybe he has nothing better to do, so he figured he'd try the family thing again. But he said he got a job, and he wants to be back with me and Anna, permanently. He wants us to give him another chance, and it's all up to me."

Jodie huffed, outraged on her friend's behalf. "Nice, putting that kind of pressure on you. Of course, you can't consider it," Jodie said.

Ginger shook her head, seeming uncertain. "I didn't think so, but I don't know. I just don't know. I should probably give it some consideration, don't you think?"

Jodie's eyes went wide. "Are *you* crazy? Why set yourself up again with a guy like that? He's already shown his stripes."

"I know. But what if he stays?" Ginger's eyes filled. "What if he means it? What if we could be a family?"

"Ginger, that's not likely to happen and you have to

make your own decision, but in my experience, people don't change that drastically," she said, sounding harsher than she meant to. She remembered all the times her father had promised her mother he'd change. He'd gone to anger management, he'd read some books, and still he took out every bad mood and every nasty thought that ran through his head on his wife and daughter.

Jodie took a deep breath, keeping in mind that she should try to remain objective, for Ginger's sake. "Maybe you can tell him you'll consider it after he's here for a year, and then you could make a decision, but I sure wouldn't just open the door and let him walk right back in."

Ginger sighed. "That makes sense. We could wait and see if he sticks around before making any kind of definite plans. Thanks, Jodie. You always seem to know what to do," she said.

Jodie wished she could say it made her feel better that at least Ginger wasn't throwing the door open to her ex, but the whole situation made her feel grumpy and irritable, and she had the sudden need to escape for a while.

"Ginger, while it's slow, do you feel okay being alone here if I pop out for a while? I have a few errands to run."

"No, go ahead. I don't have to be at the hospital today, so take as long as you need."

"I'll be back in a few hours," she promised, taking her apron off and dashing for the back door. She just had the most intense craving to see Dan, even though they'd parted company only four hours earlier. That worried her, but not enough to stay away.

DAN WAS DEEP in reading files for a colleague's promotion to tenure, and normally when he worked so intently, he wouldn't notice if the building had dropped down around him. But this time, he'd been distracted, looking at the clock, at his watch, losing his train of thought. Jodie kept popping into his mind, the night they'd shared...how his keenly honed intellect wasn't quite keeping control over his rampant emotions.

He loved her, and he knew this. He'd loved her for some time as a friend, and it wasn't much of a jump for him to fall the rest of the way.

He couldn't let her know that, of course, but withholding the truth was just a different way of lying.

Not yet, he told himself. It was too soon.

The object of his thoughts appeared in the doorway of his office, knocking softly to announce her presence. He was up and across the room so quickly he might have shifted the time-space continuum a little.

"Hey, this is a nice surprise," he said, leaning in for a quick kiss. Jodie had come by his office before, and his dorm room before that. This was the only time he considered closing the door and clearing his desk, but the obvious tension in her expression made him reconsider. "Everything okay?"

"Do you have a few minutes?"

"Sure, you're saving me from terminal boredom," he joked. Though he actually found his colleague's work very interesting, everything paled in comparison to spending time with Jodie. "You're stressed," he commented, closing the door.

"I just…it was a weird morning."

"How so?"

"It feels like everything is topsy-turvy these last few days—Bizzaro World, you know? Everything seems to be upside down."

Dan smiled. It was one of the pleasures of his life that he'd been able to nurture an appreciation of the geeky world of comics to Jodie.

"Like what?"

"Well, the bakery was robbed, Ginger is thinking about going back to her ex, and then you and me… everything is the opposite of what it was a week ago."

Uh-oh. Dan felt a spark of worry fly through the air, but quickly dashed it with a splash of logic.

"Change is the norm, Jodie. Things can only remain static for so long. It's basic chaos theory, actually," he said, the idea grabbing him as he continued to explain how there was order in apparent disorder, and stability within what was seemingly paradoxical.

"The trick, really, is not to expect that everything will stay the same. Variability is the norm, and relationships, like ours, are living, growing things—the same with Ginger, or even a business. It's all a process linked into thousands of different influences and—"

Jodie held her hand up, wincing. "Stop. Please, *stop*."

Dan blinked. It made such perfect sense. Beautiful sense, to him, which was what he loved about science and math, examining the deeper structures of—

"Dan. You can't apply science to this."

"You can apply science to anything," he said simply.

"Okay, fine, but it's not making me feel any better about what's going on. I'm still so...anxious. I don't like it. Like there are ants crawling along my skin." She shivered, rubbing her arms.

No, she wouldn't like it, Dan admitted. It was paramount to Jodie to feel in control. Her desire to control things made her a great businesswoman, but it was also one of the reasons he stayed out of the business. Jodie didn't deal well with variables. She was right, though. Logic wouldn't help a person who viewed their problem emotionally, so he asked the next logical question, based on her emotional state.

"What would make you feel better?"

She took a deep breath, looking him straight in the eye. He almost smiled. That was his Jodie—attack things head-on.

"First, I'd like to make sure we really are still just friends. Friends who have sex, but only friends."

Dan hedged, choosing his words carefully. "That was the deal." *Was* being the operative word, to his mind. "Why do you ask?"

"I don't know. Just hearing Ginger even contemplate going back to Scott wigged me out. I mean, he's been a terrible husband and father, but she said she *loved* him. I think she's making a huge mistake even considering it, but I don't think it's right for me to talk her out of it, either, not really."

"I agree, it's not your place to do that, though you

can give her your honest opinion. Friends do that," he said. "But why would her problems bother you so much? Thinking about your own dad?"

He saw her tense up considerably. He knew it was something she preferred not to have brought up, but after the length of time they had known each other, if she could talk to anyone, it should be him.

"I guess, yeah. It reminded me too much of what my mom used to say, that we had to try to *understand* my dad, because we *loved* him," she said, emphasizing the key words with a clear level of disgust. "She used to love to excuse every bad thing he did. You know, she even told me once that you knew how much you loved someone based on how much you were willing to put up with."

Dan's heart ached for Jodie. He hated that she'd been so hurt and wished there was a formula he could create, some easy fix for the deep wounds that her family had left her with. Unfortunately, even time hadn't healed them, because she kept carrying them around, holding them up as a shield. He couldn't blame her, he supposed.

"Your mom was radically unhappy and in denial. You know that. She didn't have the emotional strength that you do. You're a whole different person, Jodie."

"Oh, I know. I would never do that, to love someone so much that they could do anything, be someone's willing doormat."

He lowered himself into a squat where she sat in the chair and took her hand in his. "Do you really think that's what love is? Real love?"

"I don't know. Love seems to lead people to making terrible decisions that just bring pain, and then more pain. All you have to do is look around to see how miserable love makes people. I can barely stand listening to Ginger talk about throwing herself back into a relationship with Scott. I told her to wait him out, to see if he really sticks around before she makes any promises."

Dan nodded. "Well, that's sensible, considering his past behavior. Was she receptive?"

Jodie shrugged, then nodded. "Yeah. She seemed relieved to find a middle ground."

"So maybe she's not being as reckless as you think. And you helped. Sounds like a smart idea to me."

He saw her cheeks flush pink at the compliment. Jodie was used to being told she was hot, sexy, beautiful and any number of compliments based on her appearance, but the only time Dan ever saw her become shy was when someone told her she was smart. It was ridiculous, because she was extremely intelligent, though she didn't believe that about herself.

"You're only saying that because I'm sleeping with you," she said more jokingly, though he knew on some level she meant it.

"Well, that's more proof of your being smart," he said, nudging her back and making her smile. "Really, I wish you wouldn't sell yourself short. I knew you for a long time before we had sex, and I've always thought you were smart. I've depended on your perspective and advice a lot, if you recall."

She frowned, disbelieving still.

"Do you remember when we were picking out a spot

for the bakery, and I liked the place downtown, but you found the space we have now? The place I liked was new, clean and completely sterile, and would never have had the charm or atmosphere, not to mention the street traffic, of the spot you chose. You had a vision of what Just Eat It could be. If left to me, I would never have been able to make the business work," he said honestly.

Jodie had the ability to envision things in a way he never had, and he'd always found it fascinating. Ideas seemed to just pop out of her head, and they were almost always good ones.

"Then," he added, remembering, "you were the one who came up with the holiday marketing campaign last year, and how many times have you helped me figure out what projects would be best to spend my time on when I get overloaded and can't see the forest for the trees? You always manage to cut through the clutter," he said.

She looked away, shifting, visibly uncomfortable. "That's not smart. It's practical."

"It's also being smart, Jodie. There are different ways of being smart, different kinds of intelligence. I could never do the things you do," he added, as the hand that he had rested on her knee started sliding up and down her thigh. "And one more thing," he said, leaning in to kiss the soft skin just under her ear, enjoying her drawn-in breath.

"What's that?"

"I'm *very* smart, and I *know* smart when I see it…and it's always a turn-on. And you, all of you, including your brain, completely turns me on," he said, tipping her face toward him for a deeper kiss, because he was being completely honest. He was so turned on he couldn't think straight, being this close to her, sharing this moment.

"Well, I guess you would know," she said breathlessly as they broke the kiss and she undid the top button of his shirt.

"You know, I've never had a woman in here, in my office," he said, "for anything other than business."

"Well, Dr. Ellison, I think maybe we need to expand your horizons," she said with a sexy chuckle that made him wonder if his knees would work when he stood up, taking her with him.

He looked at her over the top of the glasses he'd worn in place of the new contacts—some habits were hard to break—and crossed his arms in front of him.

"Ms. Patterson, we do have the perfect situation in which to conduct a few experiments. Would you like to assist?" he asked.

"Of course, but what do I do? I don't know much about science," she said, catching on quickly.

"First, you should undress. Slowly, please."

"But—"

"Don't worry. I'm a doctor," he reassured her with a smile.

"Okay, then," she agreed with just the right amount of sexy apprehension.

He was ragingly hard as she took the blouse she wore off—slowly, as he'd asked—and draped it over the back of the chair by his desk. She faced him, the gorgeous swell of her breasts revealed perfectly by her lingerie, looking at the door in mock concern.

"I'm happy to help with your…experiment, Doctor, but what if someone comes in?"

"The door is locked."

She undid her jeans and slid them down one leg, and then down the other, until she was before him in nothing but her bra and a black thong.

He was pretty sure if he so much as moved a muscle he would come—having Jodie like this, here in his office, was a fantasy he'd played through many times but never imagined in his wildest dreams would come true. The impromptu role play just added to the excitement.

Her eyes never left his, and he could see she was as turned on as he was, her nipples hard already, her skin flushed, eyes hot.

"What now?" she asked.

"The next step is very, very important," he said with mock severity, stepping up closer and starting to take his glasses off, but she stopped him.

"No, leave them on. I…I like them," she said, with a bit of a hitch in her voice that melted him.

"My nerdy glasses do it for you?" he said teasingly, letting his fingers drift softly over the flat plane of her stomach.

"*You* do it for me. I've always loved your glasses. The contacts are fine, too, but I think the glasses are sexy," she said, and leaned in, taking his mouth in a kiss that proved her point.

He pulled back slightly but didn't let go. "For our experiment, I'm missing one critical piece of data."

"Which is?"

"I need to know if there's something secret, something you want that you've never done with any other man." He paused, holding her gaze. "Tell me."

She went quiet, looking away, and he wondered if he'd spoiled the moment.

"Wait a minute," she said, slipping away to go to her purse, and came back a second later with a scarf that she handed to him.

"Tie it around my eyes. Blindfold me," she said breathlessly, slightly nervous, even.

"Like this?" he said, doubling the material over a few times to make it opaque and then tying it carefully around her beautiful eyes.

"Yes."

"And now?"

He watched her swallow deeply before she said, "And now you can do anything you want, Dan."

There was no turning back for him.

How could she give herself to him like this and not believe in love? Dan vowed that one way or another, he would make her believe.

7

JODIE RELEASED THE breath she'd been holding as Dan tied the scarf ever so gently around her face, his hard chest pressing into her as he did so. She bit her lip to stifle a moan. Vulnerable, exposed and unsure, she'd rarely been this turned on.

It was a fantasy, but one she'd never dared explore with a lover. She had a small list of lightly kinky things she'd always wanted to try but had never been trusting enough to give up the control, the awareness. Now, because he'd asked, she wanted to give him this.

"Dan?" she asked, uncertain about his silence.

"Just taking you in, sweetheart...taking my time."

She smiled. "I like the sound of that."

He ran a hand up her arm and she shivered, staying still. It was another part of the fantasy, to be passive, to really let him do anything he wanted.

She gasped when his hand slipped inside the lace cup of her bra and pulled sharply, ripping the delicate sheath of fabric away from her skin, her breasts falling forth as she felt it fall away. It had been a damned expensive bra, she thought, but worth every penny to have him tear it off her.

"I'll buy you another," he growled against her breasts, burying his face in the softness there, suckling one eager nipple, then the other, then back again until she was leaning on the desk to support herself.

Her fantasy wasn't disappointing her in the least— everything was so much more of a surprise, so intense, when she had no idea what was going to happen next. And Dan was proving good at surprising her.

"You're beautiful, Jodie...I want you so much I hardly know where to start," he said raggedly, planted between her thighs, exploring the inner shell of her ear with his tongue until she was so wet she almost worried about his desk. She could feel the material of his clothes against her naked skin. He was still dressed. The friction of the fabric was erotic, and she rubbed against him shamelessly, seeking out every tactile sensation she could in the absence of sight.

He worked his way down her body, pushing her legs open wider and she felt his shoulders inside of her knees.

"Oh yes," she breathed, every nerve ending in her body waiting in delicious anticipation of what she thought he would do.

Waiting for the soft kiss that she loved, but she heard him searching for something on the desk, and the sound like a package opening. Protection?

She jumped in surprise when he touched her again, a whoosh of breath making her dizzy as he found the hard knot of her clit with...something.

"Dan...what is that?"

"A textured silicon glove. I've been testing them for the manufacturer. It hit me they could have other, more creative uses than what they're normally used for," he said, drawing his fingers along the slick center of her sex, the spongy bristles of the glove gliding over her like a hundred little fingers.

He pulled the thin strip of fabric aside, sliding one gloved finger inside and moving in such a way that she buckled, coming hard and spontaneously, pleasure consuming her.

"Oh, no, I think I was too loud," she said, panting, pushing herself up on the desk slightly.

"The secretary is out for the half day. I love it when you come like that for me," he said, petting her some more. "No reserve, no holding back."

"Like I had any choice," she said ruefully, but she smiled. She liked it, too. With Dan she didn't have to hold back anything. She didn't have to put on a show or be anything other than herself, because he already knew her so well.

He stepped away, and she mumbled an objection. She wanted more. Even after coming, she was still wired, still wanted more, wanted *him*.

"Dan?"

"I'm here, honey. Had to undress," he reassured her, stepping back in between her legs, naked now, she could tell.

"Oh, thank goodness," she said.

He pulled her up close for a deep kiss as he wrapped

her hand around his cock, stroking his length with her, their fingers woven together.

"I want your mouth on me, Jodie," he said, helping her off the desk and down to where she blindly found his leg with her fingers, smiling.

This was fun, feeling him without seeing, letting her hands drift over short, manly hair that covered the hard muscles of his legs. She learned his textures, his scent, all so much more intimately than when her eyes compensated for her other senses.

Wanting to know his taste the same way, she found him and took him inside, between her lips, drawing deep.

"Oh, yeah, like that," he said, his legs stiffening in a way that told her he was very aroused. His fingers forked into her hair, though he allowed her to control her movements.

Her hands fluttered over the backs of his legs, his butt, his balls, as she sucked and teased him to near completion. Suddenly, he pulled away, groaning. She felt dizzy from the break in contact and looked up in question, though she couldn't see him.

"Take off the thong, Jodie," he ordered in a commanding tone that had her nerve endings sizzling. She wasn't normally one to take orders, but the way he directed her made her even hotter.

She did, while steadying herself against him, and was surprised when he picked her up in one lift, wrapping her legs around him as he lowered her hard and deep onto his erection, to their mutual satisfaction.

"This is too good, I can't stop, can't wait," he said

urgently, his kiss hard and demanding, thrilling her as her body clamped around him.

She couldn't say anything, breath stolen as his hard thrusts pushed her through another orgasm before he flooded her with heat from his own. His arms were bands of steel around her, holding her in place until they finally slowed, panting and sweaty, locked around each other.

"Wow," she said, removing the blindfold and dropping her forehead against his.

"Yeah," he said, catching his breath.

He nearly dropped her when there was a hard knock at the door, surprising them both.

"Oh, sorry," he apologized, steadying her and making sure she was okay. He ran a hand through his hair and then put a finger to his lips while shaking his head.

There was no way he could answer that door, she knew. They were naked, clothes thrown everywhere. The room was saturated with the scent of warm bodies and sex.

They watched each other, frozen in place, naked and silent, and Jodie felt a giggle rise. Dan's eyes widened as he put the insistent finger to her lips this time, and she bit it playfully.

The person at the door had started to walk away, when Dan's cell phone started ringing with loud insistence on the desk. He scrambled to answer it, causing Jodie to collapse in more hysterical, repressed laughter.

She stopped laughing when she saw his smile fade, and he answered the speaker with a series of hushed mmm-hmms and finally said, "Let us get back to you, okay?"

"Dan, what is it?" she asked while pulling on her clothes, rattled by the look of concern on his face, the joviality completely gone.

"That was a newspaper reporter. He said he met with an 'anonymous source' who showed him evidence that we've been selling chemically enhanced foods at the bakery, foods that have not been FDA tested, which could be harmful to people's health. He wants to interview us on the claim, but he's going to run the story either way."

"Jason, that—"

"Prick," he finished the sentence for her, and she nodded. "We should meet this guy, turn it around, Jodie. The pheromone formula doesn't need to be FDA tested—it's much like a vitamin or an herb. But I can show him my real data, which indicates there is no harmful effect."

"This could still be enough to scare people away. Dammit!"

"Maybe it would do the opposite, you know? Create a stir, bring people in to find out for themselves? You know what they say, no publicity is bad publicity," he offered but it didn't comfort her. Businesses were too competitive in this current economic climate for her to take those kinds of chances.

Dan had put on his clothes, as well, and walked over to her, pulling her into a hug. "We'll deal with this together. Okay?"

She nodded and hugged him back though, in her gut, she had a nasty feeling that things were only going to get worse.

DAN WAITED until Jodie was on her way, and put his plan into action.

The department secretary was out for half of the day, and he happened to know, having pooked at her master schedule for the faculty, that Jason Kravitz was involved in a meeting until three.

He also knew where one of the master office keys was kept. Making his way toward Kravitz's office, he intended to find out whatever it was that Kravitz had on Jodie, to take any copies of the pheromone formula. It would be, of course, evidence that he was the person who had broken into the store. Dan could call the police, but he doubted that it would stand scrutiny, especially since he'd have to admit to breaking into Jason's office to get it. That would cause more trouble than it was worth. His goal was to minimize any damage to Jodie or the bakery, and to get Jason Kravitz out of their lives so that he and Jodie could focus on each other.

Stopping by the office, he didn't hesitate, sliding the key into place and then locking the door behind him.

Looking around, he blinked, taken aback for a moment. He'd never been in Kravitz's office—they certainly weren't friendly—and he couldn't believe what a mess it was. Paper, books, stacks of…everything were everywhere.

How did the man work this way? Dan needed

order, needed things in their place, had to be able to concentrate.

This would also make it much harder to find anything, but he started in the most obvious spot, the computer on the desk. Dan took a few stabs at cracking the password, but who knew how Kravitz's demented mind worked?

Password protected, of course. But he had to have some hard evidence somewhere, some lab reports or something indicating what he'd found when he had analyzed the cookie icing—that had to be the evidence he was showing the *Sun-Times*.

The way Jodie's face had fallen when she heard that news had broken Dan's heart, and he was determined to protect her in any way he could. Still, his plan to find the evidence in Jason's office wasn't bearing much fruit, he thought in frustration, searching through papers and drawers.

"Yes!" he said aloud to the empty room as he finally found a stack of lab reports, not completed here at the university, but tests conducted at an outside lab, off site. Dan scanned the report, nodding. This was his formula, all right.

Just as he was folding the report and putting it back in his jacket, the door opened.

"Kravitz," he said, sounding calm, though he had obviously been caught with his hand in the cookie jar.

"What are you doing in my office?" Kravitz said, his eyes narrowing to slits as he closed the door a little too hard. "Never mind, I can guess. Find what you were looking for?"

"I did, actually. Might be interesting for the police to find you in possession of lab reports on the items stolen from the bakery—and how much do I have to stretch to guess you're the one who contacted the paper, trying to ruin Jodie's business? What's your deal, Kravitz? Do you always react to rejection this way?"

Jason stood, as if pondering, and pursed his lips. "Well, I'm not rejected very often, but no. And I have no idea what you're talking about. I didn't steal anything. I could probably produce a credit card charge for cookies I bought from the bakery, and then I asked an outside lab to look at the composition of the icing, that's true—but my intention was never to hurt Jodie's business, only to help."

"Help? How exactly are you helping?"

"It's clear you never did extensive testing on the formula—what of side effects, allergies or other problems? Could your flimsy little pheromone formula interfere with people's normal hormone ratios? This is very concerning to me as a bio engineer. The public has great worries about how we alter their food. All fair questions, you must admit," Jason said equitably, making Dan seethe. "When Jodie told me about her cookies, I thought to double-check for any problems, and make sure her product was sound."

"I ran adequate tests, and the formula is completely innocuous, as you well know. However, you also know how to make it sound like more than it is, and scare people into not visiting her store, so who do you think you're fooling?"

"I can't be held responsible for people's response to

the facts, Dr. Ellison. The public has a right to know—
the cookies don't even come with an ingredients list.
Customers don't know what they are ingesting, and what
of random effects?"

"Such as?"

"Well, the sexual side effects could be dangerous all
on their own. What if someone is attacked or worse?"

Dan rolled his eyes. "Jason, you know as well as I do
that nothing in that formula will cause that response.
There is a very mild increase in estrogen and a few other
hormone levels that isn't any more pronounced than
what happens when someone has a couple of oysters or
consumes soy."

Kravitz shrugged. "And I'm sure you could tell that to
the reporter, as well, and make sure he has your version
of the facts, but—" Jason paused for effect, and Dan
really wanted to hit him "—I guess that would mean
admitting in print that your formula really doesn't do
much of anything, that it's all marketing and a placebo
effect?"

Dan didn't say a word.

"So, I guess you have a mess to work out here, but
somehow I don't think your girlfriend would appreciate
you revealing that her cookies are lies, hmm? That could
cool your relationship significantly, I would think," Jason
said with such arrogant satisfaction that Dan found his
fingers clenching and unclenching again.

"Is that what this is about? You're jealous?" Dan
shook his head.

"Hardly. She was one night's entertainment for

me—surely promising a very…energetic evening, for certain—"

"Step carefully, Jason," Dan warned, seeing red.

"I'm actually surprised you care enough to put yourself in departmental peril for this. What if I lodged a complaint about you coming into my office, digging through my papers? Corporate espionage? Academic sabotage? Things could get sticky for you, Dan," he said, visibly trying to repress his grin. "Especially considering your involvement in future government projects. You could even lose your security clearance. All for a hot piece of ass?"

Dan reined in his anger. Jason was trying to hit a nerve, and he had, but this wasn't about him. It was about Jodie, and trying to do what was right for her. Giving Jason Kravitz more reason to cause them trouble wouldn't help things at all.

"So what do you want out of this, Jason? Simple revenge? It seems beneath you," Dan said, making eye contact. "If she was so unimportant to you, why bother?"

"It's not about her at all. It's about you, my friend," Jason said, spitting the last word in a way that made it clear they were anything but, "after you undermined me on the Eastman experiments, citing every single thing that was wrong with the project, and I know it was you who kept my security clearance from being increased so that I could work on that agricultural project last summer. I am so sick and tired of you walking around here like you are the King of Science."

Dan was stunned at the outburst and shook his head,

his anger dropping away. "Jason, I had to respond honestly about the funding for the Eastman experiments. They weren't working, and they were bleeding cash out of the department. It was part of my duty here to report honestly about that. If you could have redesigned the project to be more cost-effective, then maybe—"

"Right. Like you would have given me a green light on any of that work. You know you've sabotaged me in any way you could since I started working here. You're threatened by me, obviously, but now you are the Chair, so what am I to do?"

Dan's eyes widened. "So you go after a friend instead?"

"A logical—and efficient—solution, don't you think?" Kravitz said. "Not to mention creative, but when I realized you knew Jodie Patterson, I couldn't ignore the opportunity. I had no idea you had any female friends, let alone one like Jodie—man, how have you *not* hit that until now?"

Dan kept quiet, glaring, waiting to see what the end game was, though he suspected where Kravitz was going.

"Anyway, it was a convenient coincidence. Finally I had something that I could hold over you, since it's clear you are doe-eyed over her, in love? Dan, you need to get out more. Men shouldn't fall in love with girls like—"

"What do you want, Kravitz?" Dan said through his teeth.

"I'm just hoping you can help make things go my way for a change."

"How so? How do you think hurting Jodie will help you in the least?"

"Because I will keep coming at her. I will do whatever I can to cause her trouble unless—"

"Unless what?"

"As it turns out, I'm once again having trouble finding enough financial support for a new project, one that is very near and dear to me. It would certainly benefit from a good review of the proposal, especially from someone who had been so critical of my work previously," Jason said with a gleam in his eye.

"You're blackmailing me?"

"That's so crass. We're colleagues, doing each other a favor," Jason said with mock indignation.

"The Eastman experiments were dangerous. I can't approve them."

"Even you admitted if I could improve the design of the experiments, they could be worthwhile."

Dan had said that, but he also worried about such touchy scientific material—having to do with agricultural chemicals—in the ethically shaky hands of someone like Jason Kravitz.

"I'll have to review the proposal. It's not just up to me, though. I don't think the proposal will ever make it through committee."

"You just hold up your end. You do that and, in the meantime, that reporter from the newspaper should be in touch," Jason said caustically.

"He has already," Dan said, moving toward the door before he really did lose his temper.

"Enjoy that. And know there will be more where that

came from until I get what I want, which will surely help you keep getting what you want, and help Jodie get what she wants, too," Jason said. "It works out for everyone."

"How very convenient."

"Yes. As it happens, I have a copyright here," Jason said with a smile, handing him a thick folder.

"I won't push through a proposal that's dangerous or untenable, Kravitz. Not even for Jodie," Dan said.

His scientific ethics wouldn't allow it. The projects took too much funding that could be used elsewhere, and had the potential to help or hurt millions of people. Dan wasn't about to put anyone—and particularly struggling farmers in developing countries—at risk with dangerous science.

"Listen, I'm sure she'd like to know where she stands on your priority list," Jason said. "I'll be sure to mention it the next time I see her."

Dan slammed the door hard on the way out.

Jodie was the most important thing to him in the world—except for his ethics. It was clear that Jason wasn't going to stop harassing Jodie in order to get back at him for what he imagined were past offenses, but Dan couldn't—and wouldn't—push through a bad project.

So Jason was right about one thing. Dan was in a mess, and at the moment, he had no idea how to get out of it.

GET 2 BOOKS

We'd like to send you two *Harlequin® Blaze™* novels absolutely free. Accepting them puts you under no obligation to purchase any more books.

HOW TO GET YOUR 2 FREE BOOKS AND 2 FREE GIFTS

1. Return the reply card today, and we'll send you two *Harlequin Blaze* novels, absolutely free! We'll even pay the postage!

2. Accepting free books places you under no obligation to buy anything, ever. Whatever you decide, the free books and gifts are yours to keep, free!

3. We hope that after receiving your free books you'll want to remain a subscriber, but the choice is yours—to continue or cancel, any time at all!

EXTRA BONUS

You'll also get two free mystery gifts! (worth about $10)

FREE!

Return this card promptly to get
2 FREE BOOKS and 2 FREE GIFTS!

HARLEQUIN *Blaze*™

YES! Please send me 2 FREE *Harlequin® Blaze*™ novels, and 2 free mystery gifts as well. I understand I am under no obligation to purchase anything, as explained on the back of this insert.

About how many NEW paperback fiction books have you purchased in the past 3 months?

❏ 0-2
EZVR

❏ 3-6
EZV3

❏ 7 or more
EZWF

151/351 HDL

▲ DETACH AND MAIL CARD TODAY! ▶

FIRST NAME	LAST NAME

ADDRESS

APT.#	CITY

Visit us at:
www.ReaderService.com

STATE / PROV.   ZIP/POSTAL CODE

(H-B-05/10)

The Reader Service - Here's how it works:

Accepting your 2 free books and 2 free mystery gifts (mystery gifts worth approximately $10.00) places you under no obligation to buy anything. You may keep the books and gifts and return the shipping statement marked "cancel". If you do not cancel, about a month later we'll send you 6 additional books and bill you just $4.24 each in the U.S. or $4.71 each in Canada. That is a savings of at least 15% off the cover price. It's quite a bargain! Shipping and handling is just 50¢ per book.* You may cancel at any time, but if you choose to continue, every month we'll send you 6 more books, which you may either purchase at the discount price or return to us and cancel your subscription.

*Terms and prices subject to change without notice. Prices do not include applicable taxes. Sales tax applicable in N.Y. Canadian residents will be charged applicable provincial taxes and GST. Offer not valid in Quebec. Credit or debit balances in a customer's account(s) may be offset by any other outstanding balance owed by or to the customer. Books received may not be as shown.

If offer card is missing, write to The Reader Service, P.O. Box 1867, Buffalo, NY 14240-1867 or visit www.ReaderService.com

BUSINESS REPLY MAIL

FIRST-CLASS MAIL   PERMIT NO. 717   BUFFALO, NY

POSTAGE WILL BE PAID BY ADDRESSEE

THE READER SERVICE
PO BOX 1867
BUFFALO NY 14240-9952

NO POSTAGE
NECESSARY
IF MAILED
IN THE
UNITED STATES

8

A COUPLE OF DAYS LATER, JODIE walked through the stained glass museum on Navy Pier, not ready to go back to work just yet. They'd been scrambling to keep the damage Jason was causing to a minimum. Dan was talking to the FDA while she was talking to the press, and right now she was exhausted. She only wanted to think about how it had been waking up in Dan's arms that morning. And the other day, in his office, when he'd blindfolded her. They were working together on every level, and the synchronicity between them made her thoughtful as she moved among the museum artifacts.

The intricate, colorful designs of the art glass, some hundreds of years old, reminded her of her life, in a way. So many different aspects of her existence—business, friends, family—were coming together to create one picture, although it was confusing now where it had always been clear. Some pieces were set by masters and others saved from the ravages of the Great Chicago Fire. They were all beautiful, and she came here often, just to look at them and marvel.

And think. Right now, about Dan.

It wasn't only sex between them, and she knew it. But she wasn't ready to say what else it was. Not yet. Maybe not ever. Dan had always been the one she relied on to help her process things. His intellect helped her organize the quagmire of emotions, especially regarding things from the past, which often threatened to rise up and strangle her.

She saw Dan, touched him, and she could think again. Breathe again.

Had it always been that way? She reached out to press a fingertip to one of the gold frames, pulling back when some people came up behind her, as if they'd know.

Know what? That the great, untouchable, always-in-control Jodie Patterson was more fragile, more brittle than anyone thought? That she could have doubts, worries and fears—that she might even care more than she intended, opening herself up to the very thing she swore she never would?

"Jodie?" She was shaken from her thoughts, and turned to find a woman, part of the group behind her, smiling tentatively.

Jodie blanked for a moment, and then realized who it was.

"Donna, wow, how are you?" Jodie said, not having seen Dan's sister in several years. When they were in college, she went to Dan's house for holidays and sometimes for visits over summer break, but she hadn't seen Donna, who was older and lived on her own, for a long time.

"I'm great, how are you?" Donna asked, smiling as

she motioned to her group to move on without her, telling them she would catch up.

Jodie wished she hadn't. Donna was always nice enough, and had been polite the few times they'd met, but Jodie always sensed some sort of disapproval from the woman, as if Jodie weren't good enough to be friends with her little brother.

Not having siblings of her own, Jodie thought maybe that was normal, for an older sibling to be protective of a younger one, but it still had stung at times.

"You look gorgeous, as usual," Donna said, and Jodie shrugged, smiling.

What now?

"You still working with the same firm?" she said, trying to fill the silence.

"No, I opened my own office a few years ago. Dan didn't say anything?"

So she knew that she and Dan still saw each other. Jodie wondered if Donna knew how much of Dan she was seeing recently.

"Um, you know, he might have mentioned it, but there's always so much going on, and you know—" Jodie hedged.

"I see, yes. Listen…I know you guys are…seeing each other," Donna said.

Jodie straightened her spine. "Oh, um, I—"

She'd intended to say something slightly smarter, but had no idea what to say.

"He's crazy about you."

Jodie still stared in dumb silence, and Donna didn't say anything back, but she held up her hands.

"Listen, I know he's all grown up and it's none of my business. I just hate to see him get hurt."

"I would never hurt Dan," Jodie said plainly. "He's my best friend in the world."

"I know. But you have to know he thinks of you as more than a friend."

Jodie took a deep breath, wishing a big wind or wave or something would wash up over the pier and get her out of this awkward conversation right now.

"I do. But, like you said, it's really not your business," Jodie said stiffly.

"I know, I know. Listen, I don't want to fight or have bad feelings. I just wanted to know that you know what you're doing. Dan's different. He's a relationship guy, no matter what he says, not the guy whose name you don't know who just leaves the next morning."

Jodie barked out a harsh laugh. "Wow. So nice to know your high opinion of me."

"I'm sorry, I didn't mean it that way. I do like you. I admire what you've accomplished, and even how you live your life. Believe me," she said with a sheepish smile, "there have been times I've been tempted to ask you how you manage it. I can't seem to come across a guy who either isn't married or doesn't drag me through some heartbreak."

"Oh," Jodie said, surprised.

"But I worry about Dan. I just want you to really think about whatever it is you guys have, what you're doing and what the fallout might be."

Jodie nodded, her pique deflated. "I know. I do. All the time."

Donna looked like she wanted to ask more, but reined in the questions.

"Listen, if this does work out between you two, I want us to be friends," Donna said hesitantly.

"That would be nice. But maybe we could be friends anyway. We're both professional women, we both work here. We could have coffee sometime."

Donna smiled. "That would be nice. But allow me one sisterly moment, Jodie, and let me ask you not to hurt him. Because you can. Dan has never really had his heart broken, but if anyone can do it, you can. Just keep that in mind."

Jodie opened her mouth to say something—she had no idea what. Reassurances? Rebuttals?

But one of Donna's group came back to get her, and she said polite goodbyes, leaving Jodie standing there alone again.

Well, that was an interesting moment.

Obviously, Donna still thought of her little brother as some overly sensitive science geek instead of the hot, experienced man he was. Dan could handle whatever came his way. Donna needed to give him more credit.

But a little voice was dancing around in Jodie's head now—was she just making excuses because she knew what Donna said was right?

She was taking Dan out tonight, and had to get home and get ready. In truth, she was a little nervous about it. They were meeting a bunch of her friends at a club. It wasn't something she'd planned on, but she had a night out with the girls, and they wanted to meet the new guy who had been taking up her time. Especially when they found out it was the infamous Dan Ellison she'd always talked about.

She moved along, the conversation with Donna playing in her head, grabbed a Coke from a vendor out on the pier and walked back toward her car when her cell phone rang in her purse.

"This is Jodie," she answered like she always did on her business line, though she didn't recognize the number.

"Jodie Patterson?"

"Yes?"

"You should be ashamed of yourself!"

The angry statement caught her off guard, and she froze, about to hit the button to unlock her car.

"Who is this?"

"Esmerelda James, from the South Side Retirement Center. I cannot believe that your bakery is selling cookies with drugs in them!" the indignant woman huffed. "Was this some kind of joke you thought would be funny to play on the seniors? Do you think old people don't know about these things? We ordered six dozen of those cookies for our annual picnic, and now we have to try to find something else at the last minute!"

Jodie pinched the bridge of her nose, cursing Jason silently as she let the woman's tirade wear down. She couldn't last much longer...Jodie hoped.

"Mrs. James, I assure you, there is nothing harmful or inappropriate in those cookies."

"That isn't what the nice young man who called said."

"What nice young man?" Jodie asked. Apparently

Jason had called under the guise of a local health department official, reporting the "problem" with the bakery's cookies, and the story in the news wouldn't help much, either.

Jodie had gone to talk to the *Sun-Times* reporter, but he'd obviously thought Jason's side of the story was sexier. While incorporating some of Jodie's quotes, pitted against Jason's Ph.D. and lofty scientific claims, she'd sounded ridiculous and defensive in the piece that was printed. Dan didn't agree, but he wasn't being objective.

"I wish you wouldn't cancel your order," she said, keeping a level, friendly tone. Mrs. James was not the one she was angry with. Jason must have sneaked a look at her order book while he was stealing the formula. Unfortunately, there still wasn't anything she could do to prove any of it.

He'd claimed to have bought some of the cookies and then noted some "effects" he thought were disturbing. Running a few of his own diagnostics, he had claimed to find some sort of additive or drug in the frosting, and had reported it to the FDA. She hadn't heard anything from the government, but Dan had assured her he had contacts, and would head Jason off at the pass.

Right now, she just wanted to keep from losing any business.

"I can do anything you like, and even change the frosting. There's no need to use our Passionate Hearts formula. Just let me know what I can do to make this right for you."

"Well, I don't know," Esmerelda equivocated.

Jodie swallowed hard. "Fifty percent off. And we'll throw in another dozen if you keep your business with us."

She would be selling the cookies under cost, but what else could she do?

"Okay. But if you can just give us the plain frosting, that would be preferred. The last thing we need around here is a bunch of frisky seniors," Esmerelda said wearily, and Jodie had to smile in spite of the situation.

"I promise. Thank you, Mrs. James."

Jodie didn't realize until she put her phone back in her purse that her hands were shaking.

Why was that? She'd had confrontations in business before, and they never shook her up. So why did she feel like everything was caving in?

Taking a deep breath, she got in the car and drove the short distance across town to stop by Just Eat It before she went home to get dressed for her night out.

As she pulled into her parking spot, she frowned as she saw a crowd filing out the door. What now?

Coming in through the back, she saw a harried Ginger trying to cover ten places at once, and customers waiting anxiously for service.

"Ginger, what's the deal?"

Ginger pushed her hair back into her cap, and rolled her eyes. "They all want to put in orders for Passionate Hearts before the FDA tells us we can't sell them anymore. We're sold out of everything we have, and I have more in the oven, but I can't keep up."

"You should have called—I would have come right in."

"You have a lot on your shoulders. You need a morning off, too, you know? I've kept up—just barely."

"Bonus in your check this week, my friend," Jodie said, meaning it and donning her apron.

It was madness. Some people wanted cookies right now, to stock up on, including the notorious Mrs. Mitchell.

There was a large group of new faces, people who hadn't known about her Passionate Hearts formula, and a singles group who wanted to see if her cookies could help them snag the mate of their dreams.

Jodie fielded questions, clarified misunderstandings, and took orders as quickly as she could, muttering under her breath to Ginger, "They're cookies, not miracle makers." One particularly desperate woman asked if they would help her attract the man at work she had been crushing on for a while. Even though he was twenty years younger.

There seemed to be a never-ending line of people, and when Jodie looked up to see Dan staring at the crowd in amazed wonder, she put him to work, too. The more hands the better.

Halfway through the day, it actually became fun, with three of them. She'd gotten a lot of good marketing ideas, too. Like hosting a Passionate Hearts Singles Night at the bakery, and asking local romance writers to come to the shop for signings.

Her worries about keeping up her business evaporated, as long as she could still keep selling her "magic cookies," as one lady called them.

"We can, right?" she asked of Dan as she turned the Closed sign over early and they all collapsed onto the chairs she had in the back. "The FDA or Health

Department isn't about to come in here and yank my license?"

Dan shook his head but looked pensive.

"I know that face. What happened?" she asked, dreading the answer.

"Well, I talked to my FDA contact today, and Jason is either very clever, and was trying to get us to tip our own hand or he is playing some other game, because he never reported the formula. They had no idea what I was talking about, and when I explained, my friend said he'd keep an eye out, but that it wasn't anything he thought sounded like they needed to get involved in. Jason probably knew that. He was faking us out. Empty threats."

"But why?"

Dan shrugged, though he did this funny little thing with his eyes that made Jodie go on alert. Something about his body language was off, and she couldn't figure out what, but it wasn't like Dan to hide things. Maybe he was simply tired and stressed, like she was.

"Okay, that's a relief, that we're not really under any threat from the government agencies."

"But what is Jason up to?" Ginger added, sliding off her chair, standing.

"That's the million-dollar question," Jodie said.

Dan did that funny thing with his eyes again, and Jodie flattened her lips. It looked suspiciously like guilt—but why would Dan be guilty? He was hiding something, and she was going to get to the bottom of it.

"Are you heading off to get Anna?" she asked, watching Ginger pack up.

"Yeah, uh, she's with Scott, and we're meeting for dinner."

"That's nice," Jodie said carefully. "Are things working out okay?"

"So far, so good. He's been great, but you know, I'm just letting it roll out, and seeing what happens," Ginger said lightly, but Jodie could tell from the look on her face that she was head over heels for her ex, and up to her ears.

Maybe that was okay, Jodie considered. Maybe Anna deserved her dad around, and if Ginger loved the guy, who was Jodie to say differently?

"Well, just have a good dinner. One step at a time," Jodie said, and hugged her friend, who seemed to relax. Had she been expecting something more critical from Jodie?

Come to think of it, Ginger hadn't said much, but it had only been a few days. Still it was a reminder for Jodie. She cared about her friend, but Ginger's decisions about her own life were hers and Jodie wanted to be supportive.

Ginger left, and she and Dan were alone. It took him about two seconds to pull her close and kiss the breath out of her.

"I've been dying to do that all afternoon," he said against her lips, and she had to admit to losing all train of thought.

"Don't hold back on my account," she invited, and steered his lips back to hers, enjoying another couple of long minutes of wet, hot mindlessness.

"Do you have anything else to do here? Do you still want to go out or, maybe take this party home?"

Jodie pursed her lips, studying his eyes, his face. She loved the laugh lines around his eyes, and hadn't really noticed them before. And his eyes had tiny flecks of amber in them, which reminded her of the glass.

"Jodie?"

"Hmm? Oh, yeah, sorry. No, nothing left here. We should go out. Plus, my friends are expecting us."

"Sure."

Not wanting to ruin the mood, she drizzled light kisses along his jaw. "It can wait."

"Okay. I have something I want to ask you, too."

"I bet," she said with a wide smile.

"Not that," he said, smiling. "I have to deliver a paper next week, to colleagues and a bunch of government types. I hate this sort of thing, but it's kind of a big deal. There's a reception afterward, in my honor. I'd really like it if you'd be my date for the event."

She was so surprised she barely noticed how he'd reverted, to some extent, into the "shy Dan" who had trouble asking girls out on dates when she had met him back in college. He pushed his glasses up again, and there was a slight flicker of doubt in his eyes, though it was nothing compared to the wave of self-doubt she was suddenly feeling.

"A science event? With scientists?" she asked, sounding stupid, but her brain had kind of stalled. Dan grinned.

"Yeah, pretty much. It would mean everything to me to have you there. I want you to know my world, my work. I want to meet your friends, get closer—as much as we can."

Even if she wanted to—and she did—how could she say no?

"Of course. I'd love to," she said, but Dan was the only one who was relieved by her answer. For the first time in a long time, Jodie was terrified to go out on a date.

9

IT WAS ALMOST TWO HOURS later by the time they made it to the dance and dinner club where Jodie met her friends every week—they'd gone to his apartment and hers, showered and changed.

Dan pasted on a smile for her sake as they walked into the noisy, crowded club. He'd much rather have taken a long shower with Jodie, and then spent the night inside, maybe with some takeout and a few good television shows.

But this meant a lot to her, he could tell. She grabbed his hand, smiling with anticipation.

"There they are," she said, waving to a group of women sitting at a large round table on the other side of the dance floor.

Dan hadn't really thought to mention that he'd never learned to dance. Dancing hadn't really come up between him and Jodie, so he'd never had reason to mention it. When Jodie said they were meeting her friends at a club, he hadn't thought about it. All he cared about was having a night out with Jodie.

But he was here now and thankful he'd let Jodie prod him on what to wear. His jeans were fine, and he wore a black shirt and jacket that were apparently stylish enough to pass muster.

When he'd reached for his contacts, Jodie had insisted he wear his glasses. She really had a thing for the glasses, he thought with a smile.

They approached the table where six other women popped up, alternately hugging Jodie and smiling at him, their curiosity evident as they made room for two more to sit.

"So this is Dan," a voluptuous blonde named Sylvia said to Jodie. "Well done, Jodie. Well done," she teased in such a flirtatious tone that Dan worried he might actually blush.

Luckily, the woman who sat on the other side of him, Melissa, was a computer engineer and Dan enjoyed talking to her, feeling more in his element.

As they ordered food and sat talking, Dan watched Jodie enjoying time with her friends, admiring how engaging and witty she was, how easily she could navigate the flow of conversation.

He became more relaxed, too, laughing and talking with the group of women, who, like Jodie, were all successful, intelligent people. He also found out that he was the only man she'd ever brought to dinner with her friends, something that they attached serious significance to, he could tell.

One of the women was even a chemist who worked with the company that Dan was creating his cologne for. Though he couldn't tell her about it, he was surprised to find out that she was the creator of the perfume Jodie wore.

"I love that scent. You made it?" Dan asked, impressed.

Patrice was so proud of her work, he could see it, and it was fascinating. She knew the origins of every element in Jodie's perfume, which had been a special birthday gift.

Obviously Jodie's friends thought very highly of her, too.

"So, Lynn, you run your own tattoo parlor?" he asked the woman sitting across from him, fascinated. He'd never had the nerve to get a tattoo, but as he listened to her talk about the changing perceptions of body art Dan wondered what Jodie would think of him getting one.

It was also incredibly erotic to think of some small tat, maybe a butterfly or a flower, placed on her body in a spot only he would know about.

Jodie must have picked up his mood since, as they chatted with Lynn about it, Jodie's hand danced up and down his thigh, discreetly inching a little closer to his crotch, where he was becoming increasingly aroused.

When she pretended to reach for a dropped napkin and closed her hand over him, he nearly spilled water all over the table.

"Jodie, behave," Karen chastised playfully. She was the oldest, and clearly the maternal figure of the group—literally, as she was several months pregnant.

Dan was finding something erotic about everything he looked at, and all roads led back to Jodie.

Jodie with a tattoo.

Jodie wearing sexy perfume.

Jodie round with a child. His child.

The thought stunned even him, and he cleared his throat, smiling at the woman, and standing.

"Excuse me for a moment, ladies, I'll be right back," he said, needing to process his thoughts. Suddenly the atmosphere of the club closed in a little, and he craved some fresh air.

They assumed he was heading to the men's room, but instead he circled back to the exit and stood outside the door, watching people go in and out of the place.

Doubts assailed him.

What if this didn't work out the way he wanted it to?

What if Jodie didn't want permanence, babies and the future he was imagining?

He swallowed hard, his entire body and mind rejecting the thought. He'd enjoyed the evening, and he liked Jodie's friends, he really did. But did he really fit in?

He'd gotten himself in deep here, and he had to see it through.

"Hey, sugar, what are you doing out here all alone?" a sexy feminine voice asked, and Dan didn't realize the question was being directed at him until the hot young woman in a glittering, skintight outfit sidled up beside him. She stood so close there wasn't room for a breath between them, and Dan backed away.

"Just getting some air," he said politely.

"We could go get some air together," she said, invitation clear in her eyes.

"Uh, no thanks, I'd better be getting back to my…"

group," he said and smiled as he ducked through the doorway.

When he headed to the table they'd been sitting at, he noticed they were all gone.

Frowning, he looked around, and saw one of Jodie's friends on the dance floor.

Uh-oh.

They were all out on the dance floor.

He thought he would just head back to the table and wait, but then Jodie was at his side. He hadn't even seen her walk up to him, the crowd was so dense.

Jodie grabbed his hand, smiling at him. "Hey, c'mon, I *love* this song."

Dan didn't even know the song, and the club became an even louder, more intimidating place. But he looked down at Jodie's bright eyes, and felt the sting of regret. He'd have to disappoint her. Better than making an idiot of himself and embarrassing her.

"Jodie," he said, wincing. "I don't dance."

She looked surprised, and then her expression softened. She walked up close to him, her lips against his ear. "C'mon, I'll teach you."

"Here?"

"Sure, why not?" She held his hand, dancing backward, the movement of her body sinuous under the small black dress she wore, her eyes showing a daring light. "I love to dance, Dan. Come on, you'll have fun."

He very much doubted that.

Dan was pulled along after her, into the gyrating mass of bodies, and if he had been in outer space, he couldn't have felt more out of his comfort zone.

In fact, he definitely would have felt more at ease in outer space.

Nerves kept him stiff, and not in the good way. He didn't want to embarrass Jodie in front of her friends, but he just couldn't pick up the moves that they tried to show him.

Finally, Jodie shooed them away and danced up close to Dan as a sensual song with a heavy beat started up.

"You know what?" she said, looking sultry and exotic under the low light. "You don't have to do anything but be here with me. Let me do the work," she said teasingly.

Dan wasn't entirely sure what she meant until she started doing a dance that enthralled him, moving to the beat in ways that brought her into contact with his body at every point, sliding up and then down, dragging her hands over him in a way that made him forget anything but her.

"That's it, see?" she said, smiling as she leaned in to kiss him, and Dan hadn't even realized that while she danced around—and on—him, he'd started moving to the music's beat, meeting her moves perfectly, in what he felt was the same primitive rhythm as many mating dances he'd observed in native cultures.

It was like sex with your clothes on, Dan thought, forgetting anyone else around them until they were rudely interrupted by someone who sliced between them accidentally.

No, it wasn't an accident at all. The big guy was standing with his back to Dan, and had grabbed Jodie, pulling her against him in a graphic display of dance that Jodie obviously didn't want to share. She pulled away and walked around to where Dan was again, and the big guy turned.

"Listen, if he screws like he dances, you're better off going home with me, baby," the guy said just as someone else bumped into Dan, jostling his glasses.

Dan straightened them, pulled Jodie over closer to him.

"She's not interested," Dan said levelly, turning away and taking Jodie with him.

"Maybe not," the guy said, and Dan felt his hand on his shoulder.

He acted quickly, reflexively, grabbing the guy's wrists and torquing it in such a way that the big man dropped to his knees with a shout that was mostly drowned out by the music. A few people around them looked on, but mostly they just kept dancing. Dan leaned down, increasing the pressure on the joint.

"Go. Away," was all Dan said, eye to eye with the guy who winced and whined while Dan had him in the painful hold.

Meditation wasn't all he'd learned from the monks during a stay in China after college. Six months in Tibet, away from the rest of the world, and he'd learned many, many things there. It had been his graduation gift from his parents.

How to meditate to control his biorhythms, how to speak Chinese and how to drop an assailant in the most efficient, nonviolent way possible. He hadn't often had use for those skills, but kept his practice as fresh as possible.

When the guy walked away, Dan turned back to see Jodie looking at him with undisguised shock.

And lust.

Her blue eyes were dark with desire, her breasts, rising and falling slightly, just visible over the bodice of her dress, her mouth slightly parted. All signs that she was turned on, and her need triggered Dan's.

"This way," she said, and pulled him after her. And Dan was more than willing to follow.

She led him into a large room lined with coat racks, and Dan immediately understood what she was doing—it wasn't hard to deduce as she pushed him through a thicket of coats and then brought him against her, kissing him thoroughly.

"Here?" he said when stopped to take a breath.

"Yeah, here," she said. "That was so hot. I don't want to wait until we get home. I want you here, now," she said.

Dan loved her sexy commands, but was still aware of where they were.

"But…someone could come in," he said. Though he closed his eyes and bit his tongue to hold back an exclamation when her hand slid down the front of his pants and closed around him.

"That's part of the fun," she said.

Dan knew the risk and the chance of being caught did intensify the sexual experience for some people, but he'd never tried it himself.

However, he was rock hard in Jodie's hand, and he was always willing to experiment. Backing her into the wall, he deepened the kiss and gave up his second thoughts.

They knocked a few coats from the hangers as they maneuvered in the small space, laughing and making sure they were still mostly covered as he pushed the top of her strapless dress down, freeing her breasts and tweaking her velvety nipples into hard points before going lower.

He slid his hand up under her short skirt, finding she wasn't wearing anything, which elicited a groan of approval. If he'd known that all night he wouldn't have been able to think straight.

Sliding his fingers into the folds of slick flesh, he found her clit hard and hot.

"You're already so wet," he said against her neck.

She murmured something unintelligible, clearly ready from the moment he touched her, evident as she collapsed against him with a cry of release that she muffled by hiding her face in his shoulder.

"Dan, I can't believe how you do this to me," she said breathlessly, kissing him one more time before she reversed their positions, pushing him against the wall and sliding down the front of him.

Looking up, she met his eyes. "I've never had issues with orgasm, but with you it's like I almost can't help myself," she said, which turned him on even more.

"Jodie," he breathed, unable to move as he took in the words. He'd intended only to please her, and then they could leave quietly, and finish this properly in the apartment, where they would have privacy. Where he could take his time with her.

But fast and frantic had its place, too, he discovered as she took him deeply into her mouth. His cock nudged at the back of her throat as she drew pleasure from every point in his body. Forward and out, until he didn't care where they were or who came in, as long as she didn't stop.

Dan felt his caveman impulses kick up again and wound his hand into her hair, helping her set a pace that quickly brought him too close to coming. Jodie knew his body's signals well and released him, finishing him with a few deft strokes. He watched, his breath hard and hot in his chest as he came against the softness of her breast.

It was one of the singularly most erotic things he'd ever experienced.

"Jodie," he said, unsure what he wanted to say, emotions clogging his thoughts.

"I know," she murmured with a smile and came back up to kiss him, keeping careful distance from his clothes.

Dan didn't care and pulled her in close, holding her tight and deepening the kiss until they were almost ready to go again. They broke apart, panting.

"Home?" he said.

"Definitely," she said with a grin, and looked down at his chest. "That was an expensive shirt."

"I'll buy ten more just like it if we can ruin them the same way," he said, and meant it.

Laughing, Jodie grabbed tissues from her handbag and they cleaned up the best they could, making a quick exit.

"Won't your friends want to know why you're leaving early?" Dan said, as they left without saying goodbye.

Jodie shot him a wicked smile. "Oh, they'll know." Dan was glad to be going home, but he looked forward to the next time he and Jodie would go dancing more than he ever would have thought.

IT WAS A LITTLE LESS THAN a week before the awards dinner, but Dan was a lot less worried about it. He and Jodie were getting to know each other's worlds, and enjoying every bit of it.

He took her to a science exhibit at a local museum, and she took him shopping. He took her to the planetarium—where, granted, they had missed most of the show when the room turned dark—and she took him on a food-tasting excursion.

It was his turn now. Since he had met her friends, and liked them, he figured it was time to introduce her to some of his buddies. Dan had work friends at the university, and in various areas of life, like most people did. But the people he was introducing her to today, they were special.

"Hey, I know you're beat from the deluge of customers, but I wondered if you'd want to make a stop on the way back to your place?" he asked as they left the store after a busy afternoon.

He'd been helping out more at the shop and enjoying that, too. It was the nice thing about his academic schedule—he could be very flexible. He could see why she enjoyed working at the shop. It was a very different kind of gratification than what he got from intellectual work, but no less important. She made beautiful pastries, not just the cookies, and people enjoyed them. She had regulars who came by all the time, and Jodie always asked about their families, their lives. She connected with people, and they liked her. She was extremely good at what she did, which made the business more of a success than any secret formula ever could.

She looked at him with sexy mischief. "What did you have in mind?"

He chuckled. "I'd like to introduce you to a few of my friends here, at the park."

"Sure, who?"

"You will love these guys. And they are going to think you're the cat's pajamas."

She wrinkled up her brow at his phrasing and he smiled, putting his hand out for hers as they closed up and walked along the streets of Old Town, past the quaint specialty shops and beautiful historic houses. Jodie turned to him.

"Where are we going, exactly?"

"Just over to the shore."

She eyed him speculatively, shrugging, and Dan enjoyed every moment of strolling along the street with her hand in his. They stopped to buy some drinks, and turned out toward where the busy Lake Shore Drive was between them and the sparkling waters of Lake Michigan.

People ran along the paved walkway past the looming structure of the Chess Pavilion, where he'd spent many of his off hours since living in Chicago.

"My dad taught me chess when I was three, and he

told me if I knew chess, I'd always have friends. That there would always be someone to play with," he explained. "Ended up being the truth."

"Oh, is this your chess club?"

"Yeah. They're a bunch of great guys. They have a group at the university, too, but I like this better," he said.

He'd mentioned playing chess to Jodie from time to time, and had even tried to teach her, but she didn't really get into it, which was fine. But he wanted the guys to meet her. His parents were in Florida, and they had met Jodie plenty of times, though he hadn't told them yet about the new turn in their relationship. He figured it wasn't safe to say anything until he knew for sure how Jodie felt about him. But meeting his chess friends was almost like having her meet his parents.

His entire body relaxed as it always did here by the water. Several pairs of players concentrated fiercely on their game on this gorgeous afternoon, several of them with money on the table.

Dan pulled Jodie along to a group of older men at the rear of the pavilion. Two played while four more looked on.

He glanced at Jodie and lifted his finger to his lips, until the move was made. Then another, and another in quick succession until a queen was toppled and a shout of success went up from the winner, a moan from the guys on the other side of the table.

"That was the whole game? I thought people took a long time between moves in chess?" Jodie blurted out, and Dan laughed.

"Sorry I'm late, fellas. I brought someone by for you to meet," Dan said, and all of the men turned to look, their faces lighting up as they saw Jodie.

He'd told them about her over the years, of course. He never revealed his real feelings, but his friends weren't stupid. They'd advised him from time to time, and he valued their age and their wisdom.

"Why this must be Jodie," Jerry Saunders said, standing to take Jodie's hand, which he brought to his lips in a debonair gesture. Jodie chuckled and turned a little pink.

"Jerry is the playboy of the bunch, watch out for him, honey," Clip said, pushing his way forward and breaking Jerry's hold. "You stick with me, beautiful."

Dan watched as his chess friends stumbled over themselves charmingly in their welcome of Jodie. Karl Hanover, a quiet man who sat over behind Harry, sent a quiet thumbs-up.

"You guys settle down, you're going to have to have your pacemakers reset," Harry Trumbull, the man at the table, said as he looked up at Jodie, as if taking her measure.

"You play?" Harry asked Jodie.

"Uh, no. Dan tried to teach me, but it never stuck," she said apologetically.

"Well, watch and learn, then. Dan, come on, we wondered where you were, boy." Harry, the oldest of the group and the winner of the last match, beckoned him to sit.

"Sorry. Things got crazy over at Jodie's bakery," he explained, taking his seat.

Jodie had a plethora of seats to choose, and stood looking bemused for a second, but he turned and grabbed her hand.

"Here, guys. She's sitting with me. My good-luck charm," he said, squeezing her hand.

Someone slapped him on the back and Harry sighed heavily. "Can we play now, lover boy?"

Dan grinned and nodded, and the timer was set.

For several rounds, he nearly forgot Jodie was sitting next to him, watching quietly. Except for her scent, which hit him every time a breeze came off the water, and the way her hand brushed his thigh when she moved.

Soon, however, Harry beat him in two rounds, and then Jerry beat him. Dan won a few after that, but he knew his focus wasn't where it normally was.

The guys knew it, too. They played ruthlessly and with delicious intent as they took him on, one by one. In the end, a round of drinks for the rest—their weekly stakes for whoever lost the most games—was on Dan's tab.

"They're a bunch of sweeties," Jodie said, standing at the bar of a local pub with Dan, sipping at a double shot of expensive Scotch, watching the guys argue about chess strategies. "I'm surprised, though. I never imagined you losing at anything."

Dan balanced several bottles of beer between his fingers and had Jody grab his own Scotch from the bar as they made their way back to the group. "Are you kidding me? You kill me at gin every time we play."

"I mean *smart* games. I would have thought you'd

be a chess champion or something. Harry's a hoot. He loved beating you."

"He beats me most of the time. He invited me into the group, and he knows my moves."

"Not the ones I know, I bet," she said, grinning and winking at him as they walked back.

"No, I imagine not," he agreed, pausing midway to the table. "But I'm not foolproof, Jodie, and I think you'd know that more than anyone. I botch plenty of things and, to be honest, one of the reasons I'm glad you accepted my invitation to the reception is because I absolutely hate delivering papers. I have never liked public speaking. No matter how much I do it," he said with a shudder.

"I didn't know that," she said in surprise. "Hmm."

"What?"

"I don't know. Just surprised, that's all."

"I know it's hard for you to accept that I'm not perfect. I get that a lot, actually." He tried to say it in complete seriousness but could barely repress the grin.

She moaned. "Puh-leese."

"There are so many things I guess we still don't know about each other, even after all this time," she said, shaking her head.

Dan grinned, loving how she fit in with his group. He enjoyed her friends, too.

Maybe they didn't know everything about each other, but they knew what was important.

10

JODIE HUMMED HAPPILY as she baked, feeling light and positive as she worked. Life was good. Business was good. Things with Dan were very good.

The trouble with the bakery had more or less blown over. There had been no big disruptions and business was buzzing along as always. They had lost a few customers, and she'd had to arm wrestle the local organization who listed her bakery as a stop on their local food tours into not dropping them, but overall, things were settling down.

There was an ongoing back and forth on the editorial pages in the paper where local people made some scathing and unfounded judgments, but then there were people who spoke up for the bakery, too. It was encouraging, and they had even picked up some new business.

Overall, Jason's plan had backfired, she thought with satisfaction, sliding a tray of cookies into the oven. They had taken a few lumps, but it was turning out okay.

Checking the clock, she frowned. Ginger was late

again. It had been happening more, and she was distracted when she was here. Jodie didn't know if it was because of her new romance with her ex-husband, or if she was taking on too much between family and working two jobs, but it was difficult not to be annoyed.

Jodie tried not to be judgmental, but Just Eat It was her business, and she had to have reliable help. Hopefully, whatever was happening with Ginger and Scott would sort itself out soon. She didn't want to have to be "the boss" with her friend, but if it came down to it, she would.

Needless to say, she was relieved when she heard the back door open and shut, and turned to greet Ginger, hoping to find out what had made her late, but found herself staring in wordless shock at Jason Kravitz instead.

"You! You turn right back around and get the hell out of my shop," Jodie hissed, her fingers opening and closing around the handle of a very large rolling pin.

"Is that any way to greet a guy you almost slept with?" Jason said with a sickening smile.

"Get. Out. Now."

"Jeez," he said, walking around the other side of a large stainless-steel table, putting it between her and him as he eyed the rolling pin. "I'd think twice about the rolling pin—don't want your business in the paper again so soon, do you? Bakery owner not only sells hopped-up products, but is charged with assault. Could there be a link?" he said mockingly, as if citing a newspaper headline.

"It would be self-defense," Jodie countered. Why wouldn't this creep just go away?

"Your word against mine, just like everything else," he replied without missing a beat. His eyes were trained on hers, cold and calm. How could she have not noticed before what a jerk he was? Normally, she had good instincts about men, but this time, she'd really botched it.

"Why are you here?" she asked between clenched teeth. "Were you hoping to steal something else?"

"Hardly. Maybe I'm here to ask you on another date?"

"Yeah, like that's going to happen."

"You never know."

"Oh, I know. And we've seen record sales this week. So it didn't work anyway," she said, hoping the news bit him hard. "Your sabotage didn't work."

Jason's expression was feigned shock. "It wasn't my intention to cause you to lose your business. If it was, I would have gone to the FDA directly. They probably wouldn't have done much, as your formula is harmless vegetable extracts, but it would have been a concern for your customers, wouldn't it? Of course, I knew that the news coverage and minor controversy would probably bring in as many people as it would discourage, maybe more."

"So what? You want me to thank you for defaming us? Our product?" she asked sarcastically.

Jodie was confused. If he hadn't been trying to get revenge on her and Dan, then what was his endgame? She asked him as much, and he shrugged, pursing his lips in a very unattractive way. It gave her the willies to think that she'd almost gone to bed with this guy. Or that she had thought that he was ever, remotely, like Dan.

"Well, basically, I wanted to yank Dan's chain. He's our departmental golden boy," Jason said with no small amount of derision. "He gets whatever he wants. Funding, projects, graduate student researchers…it makes me sick. Now that he's been appointed Chair, it gives him even more authority. Plenty of other scientists deserve those resources he sucks up."

"Jealous much?" Jodie said with a tight smile.

"Hardly. I'm a brilliant scientist. My work in agriculture could help feed millions, but my work is being waylaid by politics and schmoozing, and Dan is the main offender. He's the one who's jealous of me. I expect you to do something about it."

Jodie blinked. "Listen, I don't know where this is all going, but what on earth can I do?"

"Let's put it this way, I said it wasn't my intention to damage your business, but that's not to say I won't."

Jodie ground her teeth, hearing the bell ring out front.

"I have to get the counter. If you're staying, you're going out front. No way am I leaving you here alone."

"Fine, you first. I love watching you walk out of a room, you know," he said, making her wish she could avoid turning around as she left the kitchen.

It took every bit of discipline she had to wait on a couple of young women who seemed to take forever to make their choices, but finally she rang them up and returned to Jason.

"So, I believe we were at a point where you were threatening me again?" she said bitingly, her good mood down the drain.

"It's simple. I asked Dan a favor, to help push through approval on a project of mine, and he's declined the application. It was stupid of him. If he had made a wiser choice, none of this would have happened."

Jodie saw red, and held her hand up in a stopping gesture while she got hold of what he was telling her.

"Wait—you mean this was all about blackmailing Dan? You're using me and my bakery to try to make him do favors for you at the school?"

"I don't think of it as blackmail, I think of it as fair play. I have been on the unfair side of things for a while, and I want to even the playing field. You were a handy tool in trying to make that happen."

"You're the one who made the huge mistake, if you ever thought Dan would sell out, for anything. Even for me, or this bakery. You played the wrong hand, buddy," she said.

Jason's eyes widened. "You aren't the least bit upset that he would betray you, that he wouldn't do something as simple as signing over some money to a good project in order to save you more distress, and maybe even save your business? If he really loved you, don't you think—"

"Stop right there. Like you would have any notion of what it means to love someone," she accused.

She was the last one she thought would be making this particular argument, but her heart told her exactly what to say. "I would never want him to sell out on his ethics for scum like you."

In truth, though she would never let Jason see it, his words scorched her. Why hadn't Dan told her about this? Dan had been operating on a whole other level. Was he afraid to tell her what was going on because he thought she'd stop having sex with him?

No, she couldn't believe that. Not of Dan. But she also wondered why he would keep this from her, and what she was going to do now. His betrayal wasn't in holding the line with Jason, but in not telling her what was really going on. Didn't he think she could handle it?

"That's sweet, but not very practical. Are you sure he's worth risking this business for? What you've worked all these years for?" he asked with a sweeping gesture of his arm around the kitchen.

Jodie tipped up her chin, ready to fight. For herself, Dan, and for her bakery.

"And just how do you suppose you can threaten any of this? You've taken your best shot. And you're right. The FDA doesn't have any concerns about my formula. Dan already ran it by the people he knows there, so you've been cut off at the pass on that one," she said with no small amount of satisfaction.

Jason nodded, looking far too calm. "Right, but should your special formula be released into the wild, then you have a whole new set of problems. What would happen should your competitors get hold of it, or say, it just sort of made the rounds on the Internet?"

"You wouldn't."

"I have no choice. Dan seems to need a little extra motivation to push that proposal through. Sharing that recipe...that would hurt, wouldn't it? Your product would be one more overpriced cookie among a sea of them, driving down the price and making it not very special at all. You might survive, like you did before, but your signature product would be a thing of the past."

Jodie felt the blood drain from her face down to her feet, and the hand that had been around a rolling pin earlier now gripped the counter.

"You can't do that. I'd sue you. That's a patented formula, and we could take anyone who used it to court."

"Sure, you could, and rack up legal fees, more press coverage, wasted time—and meanwhile, you have no proof I stole or distributed anything, and your competitors would be selling cookies like hotcakes," he said, and frowned mockingly. "Hmm...that is a mildly humorous comparison, isn't it?"

Jodie was mute with rage. He was right, but what could she do? She walked to the kitchen, needing to catch her breath, and heard him follow her.

"So what do you think I can do about it, Jason? There's no way I'm going to ask Dan to approve your money. I couldn't do that, and he wouldn't change his mind anyway."

His eyebrows went up as he turned for the door. "That would be unfortunate. It seems to me that maybe you are far more devoted to him than he is to you, but that's your business."

"Get out," she said in no uncertain terms, her hand around the rolling pin again.

"I'm on my way. You think about it. You have until Monday," he said. "Then your secret formula won't be so secret after all."

Jodie took a deep breath as the back door slammed behind him, and she rushed over to lock it, something she should have done in the first place, but her mind had been elsewhere that morning.

Just as she did, she saw Ginger pull into the lot behind the alley, and so Jodie stood in the doorway like a mother waiting for an errant child who had come home after hours.

"Where have you been?" she asked as Ginger walked up to the door. She knew she was being less than gracious, but her mind was fried from dealing with Jason, and her emotions raw. What was she going to do?

"I know I'm late again, I'm sorry but—"

"I can't have this Ginger. I have a business to run, and I needed you here this morning. I can't keep coming in and having to guess if you're going to show up that day or not," Jodie said again, knowing she was being too severe, but she was angry and Ginger's excuses felt like one more betrayal.

One more person who put their life, their needs, their wants, before hers. One more person who asked her to understand while she shouldered the cost of it.

Ginger looked shell-shocked and exhausted. On some level, Jodie was concerned, but her own emotions were so frazzled, she couldn't make room for Ginger's at the moment.

Wouldn't it be better just to have a reliable employee she could count on? Being friends with her employees maybe wasn't the best policy, she thought darkly. All of her friendships, the one with Dan, the one with Ginger, were getting far too complicated and problematic. Still, what could she do?

Ginger shook her head, not coming through the door. "Jodie, I don't know what to say. You're right. I know I've been struggling with meeting all of these new things, the job at the hospital, finding time for Scott and Anna and working here. I've wanted to do it all, and Scott was saying he thought something had to give..." Ginger trailed off, searching for a tissue in her pocketbook.

Jodie's heart seized up. She knew something bad was coming, and she held her breath.

"He thinks I should quit," Ginger said in a choked voice, and Jodie froze.

Revved up from Jason, her emotions jangled and Ginger's quitting did hit her as a betrayal.

"Do you want to quit?" Jodie asked stiffly, her fingers gripping the doorway so tightly they hurt. How had this good day gone bad so quickly?

"No! I love working for you. If anything, I'd rather quit the hospital. It's so stressful and political there. With Scott's income, I could work here and maybe eventually start my own physical therapy business. But..."

"But you can't trust him enough to put your life in his hands that way. Not yet," Jodie finished for her.

Ginger nodded. "I want to, and I want us to have a chance, but I don't know what to do."

Jodie sighed, her temper settling down, and she opened the door wider. "Come on in. You're not quitting, but we are going to figure out how to make this work. You can't just keep doing what's right for everyone else, Ginger, and not for yourself."

Back inside, they did talk it through, and Jodie was relieved that Ginger, who had become more friend than employee, wasn't going to quit.

Ginger figured she could go half time at the hospital, lightening her load there, and keep the bakery job. She also promised to be on time more often.

And if Scott didn't like it, he could get lost.

Jodie found herself hoping they'd work it out, and was surprised at the change in her own thinking.

"Are you okay?" Ginger asked, after she'd calmed down, happier that a solution had been reached. "You looked kind of upset when I showed up."

"I...just have a lot on my mind," Jodie hedged. Ginger had enough to worry about without Jodie adding on the worry that her business could be in real danger, depending on what happened with Jason.

Being with Dan had put her in the potential position of losing everything she'd worked for. She also knew that she had spoken the truth to Jason—Dan would never compromise his ethics, not even for her. And she wouldn't want him to. She would never ask that of him.

But couldn't she at least ask Dan about it?

It wouldn't go over well, she knew, but she had to at least ask him. What happened then would, like Ginger and Scott, tell Jodie what their relationship was made of.

WITH EVERYTHING GOING ON, Jodie had almost forgotten that she had a date with Dan that evening. He'd insisted on taking her out for dinner, like a couple.

At the time, she had agreed it was a nice idea, but now, at the end of her horrible day, after thinking about everything, including what Jason had told her, she knew that she and Dan had to talk. She looked in the mirror as she put her hair up and realized how far away from "just sex" they really had traveled. And they couldn't go any further until she knew what was going on.

Sliding her dress off and throwing jeans back on, taking her hair down, she breathed deeply and settled her resolve as the doorbell rang. Dan, here to pick her up.

She pulled open the door and saw him frown. He was dressed very sharply in a handsome brown suit that couldn't help but distract her for a moment as her eyes slid over him. She knew what was under that suit, but he also looked incredible wearing it.

And he had flowers—damn.

"Uh, did you forget our date?" he asked tentatively, leaning in for a kiss, handing her the flowers.

Regret and confusion completely strangled her resolve as she struggled to maintain the strict decision she'd made mere seconds before.

"The flowers are gorgeous," she said, holding the fragrant gardenias to her nose. How had he known she loved gardenias? They also must have cost a fortune.

"Hey, are you okay? Not feeling well?" he asked, stepping inside and taking the flowers from her, laying them on the table. "We don't have to go anywhere."

She couldn't seem to say anything. It only upset her more. What was happening to her? She'd never had this bad a time setting the record straight with men who wanted too much.

But this was Dan, and whether she liked it or not, she wanted more, too. She wanted to have put on a new dress and watched his eyes light up when he saw it, and she wanted him to take it off when they got home later.

"I am such a complete screwup," was the only thing that came out of her mouth as he took her in his arms, gathering her up close and letting her cry all over his expensive suit.

"Not by a million miles, sweetheart," he said, and held her, letting her sob it out.

Why was she crying again?

Maybe it was more than the deal on the bakery being doomed? Had she allowed herself to feel anything but lust these past years?

She could almost think that must be preferable, if it didn't feel so damned good to be held, to have someone who was just there, when they didn't even know why.

"I am so sorry, Dan," she finally managed, sniffling and pulling away, going in search of a tissue.

She groaned when she looked in the mirror again, and found herself all red eyed and puffy, her nose looking like Rudolph and her hair...well, she wasn't going to go there. Putting a little cold water on her face, she blew her nose and straightened her back, returning to the main room, where Dan had taken a seat on her sofa.

"So, tell me who made you cry so I can go beat them up," he said with a sympathetic smile.

She plopped down on the sofa next to him. "That could be a little tough."

"Why's that?"

"You'd have to sock yourself in the eye."

A moment of silence, and he said, sounding understandably confused, "*I* made you so upset? How did I manage that?"

Jodie let out a sigh, and leaned on a sofa cushion, turning her head to meet his curious, concerned gaze.

"It's not you—well, kind of, but not really."

"That clarifies things. Thanks."

She nearly smiled. She was in so much trouble if the man could make her smile even on a day like this. First she told him about Ginger, and how their friendship had complicated work.

"Jodie, what does this have to do with me? Just lay it out there, like you always do. There's nothing you can't tell me. Nothing we can't work through."

She stood, throwing her arms up. "See, that's what I mean. That's the problem."

The poor man looked sincerely flummoxed.

She tried to explain. "Being friends with Ginger has made everything harder. I need to be able to be objective with employees, to assess their performance, have expectations, and fire them, if necessary, without it being an emotional disaster."

"But you didn't let her go, you worked out a compromise."

"Yes, but I could also be out of business, or unable to afford a full-time employee, and I didn't tell her that because I didn't want to lose her—as a friend. Friendship—and in our case, sex—they're a real problem when you mix them with business."

"How exactly would you lose your shop? And how does this involve me?" His eyes narrowed as he watched her, and Jodie took a deep breath.

"You know what my mom said to me once? That if she wanted anything from my father, just one thing, it was that he could put us—her—first. Before anything. That she could know she was the most important thing to him on the planet. But he never did. He was the most important thing in his universe, and he expected us to believe that, too. And yet she stuck with him anyway, always hoping that things would change."

He did turn then, his body tight with tension. "I have no idea what this has to do with us, Jodie."

"Really?" she said, knowing her words were taking her down a path she wasn't sure she wanted to travel down, but she was speaking the truth, exposing the real fears in her heart, and there was no stopping now.

"How about every time you took off on a science project, and didn't even let me know where you were off to or when you'd be back. You would just pop up in my life and expect me to be there. And I was." She gulped a breath, trying to focus. "And the times you forgot my birthday or couldn't meet me for dinner or a movie because you were too wrapped up in some work? Or how about now? I've worked damned hard all of these years, building that bakery up to what it is, and yes, you gave me the chance to do it, but I made it what it is. And if something goes wrong, I'll be the one who loses everything," she said.

He took a step forward. "Jodie, do you really think

I would take the bakery from you even if we broke up?"

"No. But you wouldn't do whatever it takes to save it, either, would you?" she accused bitterly.

"What do you mean?"

"I talked with Jason today. I know you denied his research funding, and he's going to sell the icing formula to my competitors, or put it up on the Internet so anyone can make it. And when he does, I lose the biggest profit-maker I have. It might kill business. Maybe all of it," she said, letting her anguish overtake any final words.

11

DAN WAS STRUCK DUMB. "Jason came to see you?" he said, unable to really get his mind around everything she was telling him.

"He came by the bakery earlier. He told me he'd never intended to go to the FDA, but that he was trying to blackmail you into approving some funding for his research, and since you hadn't, he was going to publish the formula and undercut my business."

"But that's so stupid. We'd sue."

"Sue who? We still don't have any solid proof he's done anything, and I can't afford the kind of legal fees he would cause by fighting me. He said the only way he'd change things was if you changed your mind and approved his project. Which I knew you wouldn't, so I guess that's that."

"And you took this as disloyalty, Jodie? That I didn't give in to his threats?"

She shook her head, running her hands through her hair. "No. I just wondered why I didn't know about any of it. Jason was able to blindside me because I had no idea that he was blackmailing you. I didn't know why you wouldn't tell me. No matter what, I'm the collateral damage and that's true, because he knows how we feel about each other. If we didn't have a relationship, he never would have thought he could use me against you...."

Dan held his hand up and closed his eyes as if for patience. "Wait. We had a friendship long before we had sex, Jodie. Do you think you'd be calling off our friendship if all of the same things had happened? You were dating Jason when I got back into town, so there was a good chance he would have found out about us knowing each other no matter what."

"No. He would have been a one-night thing, just like all the rest. He never would have known your connection to me...if we hadn't gotten together. It's given him ammunition."

They were silent for a few long moments. Dan was struggling, trying to sort out what Jodie was saying, about who was to blame for what. It wasn't easy, especially when his own emotions were so deeply involved. But he knew he'd do anything to keep her from calling it quits on their relationship.

She also had a point—a convoluted one, but still a point. He had put himself and his work first for many years. So had she. As friends, it was how they operated, and he'd never guessed that she felt slighted.

"So do you wish that?" Dan asked quietly. "Do you wish we'd never gotten together?"

Jodie looked stricken, and shook her head.

"No. I mean...no, I like us together. I just...I don't

know what to think. This shouldn't be a choice between you or the bakery, but it comes down to that."

"Maybe. Listen, I'm sorry I didn't tell you. I just thought you had enough to worry about, but you're right, I should have. I'm sorry for that."

She nodded, but didn't say anything.

"You never told me you wished I would have been better about contacting you when I was out of town. And I'm sorry about your birthdays. You just never seemed to attach much importance to those kinds of things. You were always out with your friends, partying, or with some guy. I have to admit, I didn't think you even noticed what I was doing."

Jodie looked surprised at his admission. "I didn't because it's not what friends do. Those are the kinds of expectations lovers have, not buddies. I have a lot of friends, and they come and go, and I don't necessarily know where they are or expect them to remember everything," she said. "But with you, it was different."

Hope soared again, and he winced at how easily she could make it happen with just a few words.

"Different how?"

The wary look entered her eyes again, but then faded to something else as she sagged down to sit on the sofa, her head in her hands.

"You and your stupid, freakin' logic. I just admitted that I've thought of you as more than a friend for quite some time. How stupid am I? I never even saw it myself. Hell, I was dating Jason as a way to fantasize about you. I never have felt this way about any of my other friends. Only you."

Dan couldn't help but grin, even in the midst of their serious conversation. His heart lightened.

"I've only ever felt this way for you, as well, Jodie. Only for you," he said, echoing her words. He joined her on the sofa.

She said nothing, just sat there with her hands over her eyes, her fingers forked into her bangs, quiet. He supposed while the realization of her feelings was a good thing for him, he wasn't sure how she was going to handle it.

"Jodie, are you okay?" he asked, unsure if he should touch her but unable to stop himself from putting his hand on her back, rubbing softly, to comfort more than anything.

"This is so screwed up. I don't know what to do," she said miserably, but he took it as a good sign that she let him pull her in close, resting her head on his chest.

"Listen, I'm sorry I blew this out of control. I thought I could handle it myself, and I never imagined he would go to you directly."

She looked up at him, her blue eyes blurry and tired from tears. He hated seeing her like this. If Dan had his way, he'd make sure she never had another miserable moment in her life, especially because of him.

"I'm sorry, too. I should have known it wasn't that you were putting yourself before me, but I couldn't help that gut reaction. I can't see what choices we have. Either you compromise your ethics or I lose my bakery, or at least, I lose the signature product we offer."

Dan kissed her forehead and sighed. "Well, some of this really *is* my fault. There are a few other things

I didn't mention, and it probably made the situation worse."

"Like what?"

"Well, for starters, I broke into Jason's office looking for proof he'd stolen the formula, the orders, and he caught me. I think it—"

Jodie jerked her head up so quickly that she nearly hit his chin with her head, and she stared at him in surprise.

"You did *what?*"

He shrugged, worried he had admitted something that was going to make it worse, but the cat was out of the bag now.

"He was in a meeting, and I thought that I could break into his office and see what I could find, maybe I could grab the information, at the very least, he'd no longer have it, or I could call the police and show that he'd stolen it," he explained quickly, wincing. "Though that didn't really make much sense, I guess, as he could have said I planted it. I wasn't thinking of that at the time."

Jodie nodded, watching him closely with a curious look in her eyes. "Yeah, but it doesn't matter."

"It does. He caught me, and that ratcheted things up. That's when he made demands for me to approve his research. I don't know that he was actually thinking of it until then. So once he knew he had me over a barrel, he decided to up his game, see what he could get."

"Dan, that's not important."

"Oh…no?"

"No." She smiled a little for the first time since he'd walked in the door.

"You risked a lot—doing something like that in your workplace and then getting caught. Your reputation could have been seriously called into question, right?"

"Probably not that serious, but it would have raised some eyebrows."

She shook her head in wonder and then leaned in to press a soft kiss, salty from tears, to his mouth. "Dan, you thought with your heart, not your head. Logic didn't matter. You weren't worried about the consequences— you were just trying to help me. You were thinking of me before everything," she said, leaning in to kiss him again, and his blood warmed.

"I—I hadn't thought of it like that," he said against her mouth. "But I guess that's true. I love you, Jodie, and I might as well say so. You have to know that's how I feel, and how I've felt for a while," he said, knowing he was taking a huge risk. "I want so much more than sex from you. I want everything. All of it. With you," he said, staring into her eyes.

She didn't pull away.

"I know, Dan. I know that now. I just…I'm afraid. I can see, in my head, how we're different from my parents, but my emotions, at the gut level they still make me react…stupidly."

"No, not stupid. You really need to stop using that word. You're being honest, and you've had pain. I know that. I don't ever want to cause you more."

"You don't. I mean, we should have been keeping each other in the loop on this, figuring it out together, but I know I don't always make things easier. I shouldn't have let Jason get to me." She shook her head. "I never want to hurt you."

"You couldn't." He knew that was a lie, but he wasn't going to have her carrying this worry around.

Her smile slanted slightly. "Not what Donna thinks."

"Donna?" He frowned. "What does she have to do with anything?"

"I bumped into her. It was fine, a little awkward, but she made it clear she doesn't think I'm right for you."

Dan's mouth flattened. "I'll talk to her."

"No. It's fine, really. She was just concerned for you, and she just doesn't want you hurt."

"I'm not a child. Donna was always overprotective, and she needs to know when to butt out."

"Well, it's nice that she cares that much for you. You have a great family," Jodie said a little wistfully.

"I know. I just wish they knew when to back off. Granted, they had a lot of challenges helping me deal socially with being so advanced, but right now what's between you and me, well, it's only between you and me."

Jodie smiled. "Yeah, that's true."

She kissed him again, a little more heatedly, and though his desire leaped, he couldn't deny disappointment that she hadn't reacted to his declaration the way he'd hoped. But maybe it was baby steps.

She'd admitted they had more than sex going on, and that she'd felt even more than friendship for a long while. Still, as her hands started exploring him, he had to back away.

"While it's hard to say no," he admitted with a groan as her teeth nipped his earlobe, "I think we shouldn't do this right now."

"Why not? I think we've said all we need to say for the moment," she said with a sexy smile.

"It's not that I don't want you, believe me. I want you constantly, but I don't want us always turning to sex to solve our problems."

She smiled. "You just have no idea how good makeup sex can be."

"Can we find out later? We were going to go out on a date, and I think we should."

She blinked. "You still want to go out?"

"Sure. Why don't you get dressed and I'll make some new reservations. We'll go out, talk, and maybe we can come up with some solutions to this problem together?"

She nodded, then readjusted his tie. "Okay. We'll go out. As long as you let me take this tie off later, and put it to some very interesting use."

His cock turned hard and her wiggling against him didn't help. He swatted her backside playfully. "It's a deal. Get off me, vixen, and go get dressed."

She was smiling, too, as she headed off to the shower.

Dan pursed his lips, an idea forming. After he called the restaurant for new reservations, he looked up another number. There was a man he'd worked on a project with a while ago—a hush-hush corporate security kind of thing—who might be able to help them.

"Hi, Kevin, Dan Ellison here."

"Hey Dan, this is a surprise. Calling to take me up on the job offer?"

"Afraid not, but if I ever get tired of academia, which could happen anytime—" they both laughed at that "—then you'd be first on my list. I was wondering if I could talk to you about a problem I have...."

"Sure, shoot."

Dan gave him the outline about being blackmailed, and the two men talked about it. Dan heard Jodie's shower shut off and by that time, he had his solution.

Now he just had to see if she was up for it, too.

JODIE COULDN'T BELIEVE that only a few hours had passed since she was alone in her apartment planning to end things with Dan and feeling like crap. Now, on a warm autumn night, she was in her favorite blue dress and heels, sitting at an outdoor tapas café that provided a great view of the river and city streets. She and Dan fed each other bits of tomato and watermelon salad. Next, they'd be trying succulent meats and cheeses from the plates they had ordered. Jodie loved tapas for the variety. You never had to choose just one thing for dinner, but could make a meal of several different kinds of foods.

She'd felt the same way about her love life, really, until just this minute. Dan filled her up and, as he pushed a piece of tuna tartare through her lips, she sucked the tip of his finger in with it and loved how his eyes darkened in reaction.

He'd said he loved her. She hadn't said it back.

She wanted to, but she couldn't bring herself to say it. Not yet. She knew once she said that to Dan, there would be no turning back. Other people seemed to fall in and out of love like they caught colds, but she'd never said that to anyone, not in the serious, romantic sense. She didn't know how to be sure that this was really love and not something else. Something that might slip away.

Thankfully, Dan seemed willing to wait.

Until then, she could try to show him how she felt for him in every way she could.

"Do you want dessert?" Dan asked as he paid the check. Jodie offered to split, but Dan had simply glared at her. She let him pick up the check, enjoying his traditional bent.

"Maybe after a walk? I know a late-night place that does great espresso and chocolate cake."

He smiled, taking her hand as they walked out to the sidewalk, heading across the street to walk along the river. "Sounds like that could keep us awake all night? What will we do?"

"Oh, I'm sure we'll think of something," she answered in the same teasing tone, tugging at his tie. She squeezed his hand. "Thank you for talking me into going out. This was perfect."

"You're more than welcome. We should make a habit of it. You look beautiful, by the way, if I had failed to mention it earlier. Everything about you is perfect, Jodie," he said sincerely.

She smiled, overwhelmed with his praise. "Don't put

me on a pedestal, Dan. I'm so far from perfect it isn't funny, and if anyone knows that, it's you."

"Well, maybe I love all of the imperfections, and so that makes you perfect—for me," he countered with logic that made her chuckle.

It was necessary lightness after the arguments and intense emotions they'd been through earlier. Getting their feet beneath them again, finding their balance.

Still, as they walked, she couldn't help but start to let some of the problems of the day leak in.

"You're worrying," he said, perceptive.

"A bit. Ginger is making a job decision, and I wasn't a hundred percent honest with her."

"It will work out. There's no way we're letting Jason damage your business."

"I hope so. I hate to mention it, to spoil the evening, but what are we going to do about him?"

Dan drew in a deep breath.

"I have an idea. I didn't want to ruin our dinner talking about it, but I think the thing we need is some leverage, to keep him from doing any more damage. I have a thought on how we may get that."

"You broke into his office and couldn't find anything. I can't prove he came to the bakery and threatened me. He's got us up against a wall, and he knows it."

"Then we just have to get creative," Dan said, lifting her hand to his lips to kiss her fingers, sending shivers down to her toes.

"You're good at being creative, I'll hand you that," she said, not thinking about Jason, but about getting home and getting very creative with Dan.

"Hey, don't distract me—until later," he admonished, settling his hands on her hips where their abdomens pressed against each other in the most inviting way. Jodie could feel he was at least halfway distracted, and loved how easily she could turn him on.

"Okay, so what's your evil plan?"

Dan sighed. "Okay, if we must. I talked to a guy earlier, while you were in the shower. He's meeting us in the morning, or I can meet him, if you're busy, but his company experiments with specialized listening equipment."

"Like bugs and that kind of thing?"

"Yeah, but very high-tech kinds of stuff. He might be able to give us a hand with this. Maybe lend us something that could help us trap Jason."

"You want to bug Jason?"

"Yeah. Maybe we can get him to confess or at least threaten you so we have proof. Then we have some leverage. We don't even have to take it to the police. All we need is him knowing we have it, so he'll leave you alone and keep the formula to himself. But we need something that will really keep him in line. I haven't worked that part out yet."

Jodie blinked. "Wow. This is kind of sexy, Ellison."

"Glad you think so. Maybe I should tell you about my government projects sometime if that kind of thing turns you on," he teased.

"Everything about you turns me on," she said, feeling vulnerable making the admission. "But I can't imagine how we'd get Jason to confess to anything. If I'd had a bug in the bakery the other day, maybe that would have helped, but I don't."

"We'll find a way."

"We only have two more days."

Jodie nodded. "So it's like wearing a wire?"

Dan started moving again, walking, his hands moving in gestures as he explained the technology. She couldn't help but grin at how geeked-out he could get at this stuff, and of course she didn't understand most of it. She did listen, though, and one thing became very clear to her.

"I know you do a lot of important work, and I don't ask about it because I figure most of it's over my head, but also, I know a lot of it is secret, government stuff," she explained. "But I'd like to hear more about what you *can* tell me. I want to know more about what you do. I bet your projects save a lot of lives, don't they?"

"Some of them, yeah. I'd like to think so. Though they aren't really my projects. I help out, offer what I can to the team," he said, and she could tell he was uncomfortable with her admiration.

"It's pretty damned noble, no matter what. I was selfish, thinking only about how much I missed you when you weren't here, but you go lock yourself up for months at a time, and help people you'll never even meet. That's awesome, Dan," she said, meaning it.

"Well, thanks. I would love to tell you more sometime," he said huskily. "Knowing you admire my work means a lot," he said, turning her to him. "It means everything from you."

He walked her slowly backward under a tree where

colorful leaves scattered around them in the wind, and their kisses turned hot. The cold, rough surface of the tree's bark was a stark contrast to the hot form of his body against hers, and she enjoyed being in between.

Jodie found she was even more aroused by thinking about Dan and his work, and how incredible this man was who could also make her knees turn to water with one touch.

They pulled apart as a family of tourists out for a late-night stroll walked closer.

"Makes me feel like my life's pursuit of baking cookies is so silly," she said gustily, with a sideways smile as they began walking again. "And being so worried about it. It's pretty lame, I guess."

"No way. Your work makes people happy on a daily basis. I'm not sure there is anything more important than that. People can be having a miserable day, come by your bakery and feel better. You can see that in your customers and how much they appreciate what you do. Don't play that down. We're all good at different things. You're creative, and you're a nurturer."

Jodie stopped in her tracks. "A *nurturer?* Are you out of your mind?" She laughed. No description was ever further from her idea of herself.

But Dan, apparently, was serious. He continued. "You take care of people. You feed them, watch after them, care about their problems. It doesn't mean you're a doormat—you're anything but that—but I would probably have wasted away in school without you. They would have found me one day a dry pile of dust at my desk," he joked, but she could tell he meant it.

"The people at the bakery know you care, too, and that's what keeps them coming back. It's why you became friends with Ginger and worried over her problems. It's why you were so upset with her, and feel so bad now. You connect with people, Jodie, and you have a brilliant way of sensing what they need and how to deliver it. Which makes you crazy good in bed, by the way," he said with another grin.

She wanted to rail against his comments, but his perspective gave her an entirely new view of herself.

She'd always seen herself as, well, a sexy bitch. Determined businesswoman, seducer of men. But a nurturer? It would take her some thinking to get her mind around that.

"Well," she said with a soft smile. "I do like that last part. Maybe we should head back to your place, and I could nurture you a little?"

"Just a minute. I want to pick up something to bring back with us," he said mysteriously, pulling her with him into a small dessert and coffee shop.

Jodie saw him go directly to the counter, where he ordered two raspberry croissants and a jar of the shop's signature chocolate sauce.

"Mmm. That will be wonderful, the sauce on that pastry," she said in approval as they took their purchases and left.

Dan smiled slightly, his look warm and promising. "Who said it's for the pastry?"

Jodie's heart just about stopped in place, and Dan smiled wickedly as he hailed a cab to take them back to his apartment.

"Mind spending the night at my place?" he asked.

Jodie eyed the chocolate sauce. "I'd love to."

They couldn't keep their hands off each other in the cab, but when they got to Dan's place, Jodie was surprised when he stopped her as she tried to tug away his jacket, wanting to get him naked as quickly as possible.

"I'm not complaining, believe me, but it's usually been fast with us," he said, framing her face with his hands. "I guess we've been making up for lost time, or wondering how much more time we'd have," he said, looking at her so intently that she shivered from the intimacy of it.

"Sometimes fast is good," she said, pressing a kiss into his palm.

"It's all been good. Every second of it. But tonight, we're going slow. We had our date, and took our time over dinner," he said huskily. "Now I plan to take my time over dessert."

Jodie's heart actually slammed in her chest. She was worldly, sexually experienced, but the way Dan was looking at her—like she was the dessert—made her feel vulnerable and unsure what to expect.

"I love you, Jodie," Dan said against her lips, "and I hope you don't mind me saying it. Or showing it, because that's what I intend to do tonight."

"No, I don't mind at all," she said on a whisper, wishing she could say the words back, but knowing that accepting his love seemed to be enough for Dan at the moment.

He led her into the bedroom, and she gasped at the sight she found there.

Champagne chilled in a bucket, and there were rose petals on the bed. Dan smiled, lit several candles and then turned off the lights. He picked up a remote, and soft music played in the background.

He took the chocolate sauce out of the bag and set it on the side of the bed.

Jodie caught her breath long enough to say, "You did all of this?"

"Do you mind?"

"Absolutely not. It's beautiful."

She was used to one-night stands and the quick, frantic sex that happened when things were just about sex. No one had ever done anything like this for her before, and she registered an emotional tightness in her throat that she had to fight back.

"It's so…romantic," she said, still taking it all in.

This wasn't just about sex and, surprisingly, that was okay with her.

"Come here." Dan stood by the huge bed looking so handsome she felt like she had been lifted out of real life and into a fairy tale.

She walked over to him, happy to comply. He seemed so unlike her usual Dan. Commanding, sexy and in control. She wanted to do whatever he said, and gladly.

All she wanted was to please him, to be deserving of his love.

"Turn around," he said softly, and she did. He eased the zipper of her dress down, pulling it gently from her shoulders and easing it down to her feet, where she stepped away from the pool of fabric.

She heard his sharp intake of breath as he ran a finger along the small of her back, tracing the pattern of the dark blue lace of her panties. She shivered under the light, teasing touch.

"I bought these just for you," she confessed. "For tonight."

No one else had ever seen them on her. No one else ever would.

"I'm glad you decided to wear them after all," he said, raining kisses along her shoulders and down her back, nibbling all the way down as he pushed the lace to the floor, as well. Jodie was trembling for the caresses, but stood in place. "You're so beautiful."

He worked his way back up her body, slowly, and undid the bra, letting it fall away. He walked around her, taking her in in a slow, purely male perusal before he faced her, still completely clothed.

She could see the possessiveness in his gaze, and it made her even hotter. He started to say something, but words failed. For her, too.

Instead, he kissed her, and she moaned as her sensitive nipples rubbed on the fabric of his suit. It was wonderful, but she wanted him naked, too, and said so.

"In a little while, don't worry," he said. "We have time."

He bent and slipped his arms under her back and knees, picking her up and carrying her to the bed, where he laid her down.

"Aren't you going to join me?" she asked, as he was still dressed.

"I just want to remember every second of this night," he said, undoing his tie, and then slipping out of the rest of his clothes, leaving the expensive suit in a pile on the floor as he reached for the chocolate sauce.

"I'll be back in a second," he said, pausing, then he left the room.

Jodie frowned, wondering what he was up to, but she heard the hum of the microwave and smiled.

He reappeared in the doorway, the warmed, open jar of chocolate sauce in his hand.

"I told you I planned to take my time over dessert," he said. His weight on the side of the bed, he dipped a finger into the jar and considered where to start.

Each nipple was treated to a gob of warm chocolate, which he thoroughly sucked away, leaving her writhing.

He painted a chocolate path down the middle of her belly, and lower, following the path with his mouth, licking every bit of sweetness from her skin, but denying her the satisfaction that she craved.

"You're evil," she said as he rolled her to her stomach. He gave the same treatment to the length of her spine, and continued to kiss and lick chocolate from the backs of her thighs and the tender hollow of her knees.

"Dan, I can't take this anymore," she said, half laughing, half warning him. "Make me come, or I'll have to take matters into my own hands."

There was a pause, silence.

"I wish you would. I'd like to watch," he said, and

she smiled, realizing what he was asking for, and she was more than happy to comply.

Rolling back over, she propped herself up on the thick bed pillows and met his eyes as she dipped her own finger into the chocolate sauce. She had some control now, and planned to tease him exactly the way he'd been torturing her.

She worked her nipples with chocolate-covered fingers until she saw Dan's nostrils flaring, his jaw tense, erection jutting in her direction as she lifted a breast and licked the chocolate off herself, never dropping her eyes from his.

Letting her thighs fall open so that he could see everything, she trailed her fingers down between her legs, unabashedly stroking herself to a swift climax that shuddered through her, but was hardly enough to satisfy.

Dan's expression was so wrought with hunger, she nearly purred. She knew he wasn't hungry for chocolate. To see how much he wanted her and to see the love he had for her reflecting in his eyes, she was humbled.

Holding her hand out to him, she pulled him down to her. "I need you, Dan," she said, and hoped he heard all of the other emotions she held underneath the words.

"I need you inside of me as deep as you can go," she said tremulously.

He accommodated, pulling her calves up over his shoulders and thrusting forward, filling her without hesitation.

"I love you, Jodie," he said as his arms slid around her, and she held on, too, her hands tight on his shoulders as he drove into her, then stopped, holding her still, his body buried to the hilt in hers.

"Dan, please," she begged, trying to move but the position he had her in, and his weight, held her captive.

"Slow, Jodie," he said thickly.

He was as good as his word, delivering long, slow thrusts and pausing between each in a way that built the pressure in her body until she felt a tear slide down her temple, she needed the release he promised so badly. She was begging now, and he smiled as he relented, driving into her with a few quick, hard strokes that pushed them both over a shuddering, incredible edge.

"I think slow is very, very good," she said as he came down beside her and pulled her into his arms.

"I have to agree," he said, hugging her close.

Jodie wished she could tell him what she knew he wanted to hear, but for now, she'd just do her best trying to show him all of the things that she couldn't seem to say.

12

"ARE YOU GOING TO give me that soap or hog it all for yourself?" Jodie asked, looking at him as they crowded into the shower together. It was a small space, really built for one, and he was okay with that as hot water poured down over the two of them.

Jodie's slicked-back hair and wet, gleaming skin made her look like something straight out of a fantasy, a sex goddess right here in his shower.

He smiled. She was making his logical mind take some interesting imaginative flights lately.

"I think I'll hold on to it," he said, pulling her up against him with his other arm, his cock hardening at the contact with her soft skin. It would seem against the laws of physics how she could excite him this way after the night they had shared.

"Oh," she replied against his lips as he smoothed the soap over her, washing her with his hands as he slid the fragrant soap over the curve of her back, the round globes of her backside. Oh, how he loved every inch of her, how her breasts jutted up against his chest, her nails sinking lightly into his shoulders as he nibbled on her neck while he continued soaping her down.

But her ass drove him crazy. So perfect and soft, he couldn't keep his hands or his eyes off it. He might be one of the brightest minds in science, according to several journal reviews, but Jodie made him revert to his primal instincts, and he loved it.

Turning her, he kept her close and soaped her front, too, letting the water rinse down over them both. As he massaged her breasts in a way he knew she liked, he rubbed his cock over her buttocks, whispering raw words in her ear, letting her know what he wanted to do, and hearing her sigh as he bent her forward against the wall. He wrapped his hand in her wet hair to gently tug her head back for a deep, hot kiss as he slid inside her body.

"Hard this time, Dan," she commanded in a sexy, purely female tone that he couldn't resist.

Any pretense of showering or washing was lost as he thrust into her, giving her what she asked for, enjoying the way the hot water washed over them.

She responded as much to tender and slow as hard and rough, and he found himself challenged to find new ways to please her. Everything between them pleased him. Dan wasn't sure a lifetime would be enough time to explore everything he wanted to do with her.

He drove himself into her, passion powered by emotions that were too strong to be expressed any other way. Her body tightened around him as she pushed back from the wall against him, fucking him back as she came with a shattered cry. Her body buckled forward and the coiled tension of her muscles pulled a mind-blowing orgasm from him, as well.

He didn't want it to be over. But when it was, he pulled her against him and they stood under the water for a moment, quiet.

"How is it possible that it just seems to get more intense?" he asked, planting kisses on her neck. "I love you so much."

There must be some kind of algorithm for this somewhere, he thought, and if not, he was going to write one. There might even be a paper in it. He was pretty sure the scientific community would be shocked, and it made him smile to consider actually doing it.

"I know. For me, too," she said against his chest, and he felt the familiar pang of his unrequited sentiment, but he was willing to give her time. He needed to hear the words, but told himself that, for now, this was enough.

He knew what she felt. He could see it in her face and feel it in her responses to him. She'd agreed they had more than sex between them, but she still had to work out some things before she could open her heart completely.

He could wait.

Stepping out of the shower, they toweled off and grabbed robes from the back of the door. His guest robe had never been used. He didn't bring many people to his home, since it was his retreat, his place to be alone and away from the demands of the world.

He wrapped her in a towel and pulled her up close. He had to teach in an hour, and for the first time in his life, work wasn't the first thing on his mind. It hadn't been for days. Being with Jodie, and knowing that he wanted her in his life, meant more to him than anything.

"Listen, Jodie, I've been thinking…"

"Hmm?"

"With Jason, I'll talk to the committee again, and see what I can do. It's just not as important as making sure you're okay."

"Two can play that game, Ellison. I won't let you sacrifice your ethics. We can let Jason take his best shot. But the more I think about it, the more I think he's wrong. We may lose some of the uniqueness of the Passionate Hearts, but the bakery will survive. I won't let anything else be the case," she said, sounding and looking resolute.

Dan's heart flooded. He was aching to hear the words from her, that she loved him, but what she was saying amounted to the same thing. She hadn't said the words, but she was willing to put everything she had worked for over the years on the line for him. His own resolve returned, wiping out doubt, and he kissed her lightly.

"We'll figure something out. I promise," he said, and he meant it. There was no way he was putting Jodie in the middle of this, putting her, or her business, in any more danger. He'd handle it himself, even if it cost a tiny chunk of his integrity to do it.

He'd put his own needs first for too long. Now it was all about Jodie.

It was a gorgeous day. Fall was her favorite season, and it was just starting to really nip at the air in earnest. Not all of the leaves had changed yet, but as Jodie sat at the pretty café near the Lincoln Park Zoo, she enjoyed watching some of the bright red pop out, and was relieved that the summer heat was passing.

She tapped her foot nervously on the floor. The server had come by twice asking her if she wanted to order, and as time passed, she thought that maybe Ginger wouldn't show up. Finally, she saw Ginger rush through the door, hurrying across the café to her table.

"I'm so sorry I'm late, again, I know," she began but Jodie put up a hand and then, before she could say anything, stood up and hugged Ginger.

"Don't worry about it. How are you?"

Ginger looked relieved. They ordered their food quickly, barely reading the menus.

Jodie took a deep breath. "Ginger, there's something I didn't tell you the other day," she said, but as she finished the sentence, her throat tightened and her eyes stung.

It surprised her. She wasn't typically a crier. She'd learned young that tears only aggravated her father and made things worse, so she'd thought that she'd all but trained crying out of her emotional repertoire, but tears certainly were a reflex these days. "I'm sorry, I'm pretty stressed—" Jodie went on to tell Ginger about Jason, and the chance that their business could be in trouble.

"So I don't know that I'll be able to guarantee the bakery job, depending on what happens. The recession has already hurt a bit, and if he does manage to damage our business, well…I don't know. I should have told you, but I didn't want you to quit."

"Oh, honey," Ginger said, "you couldn't get rid of

me if you tried," her voice high and tight as she fought off her own set of tears, and before the food came they were both weeping and laughing about it, and Jodie knew then everything was going to be okay.

Taking deep breaths and sitting back down with the air less tense between them, Jodie smiled at the waiter who smiled back in *that* way, pausing for a moment longer than he had to and refreshing her water though it had barely been touched. He was cute, she supposed, but she could have cared less.

"I was worried, thinking you would make the decision to cut back on your hospital hours when I didn't know what was happening with the shop..." Jodie proceeded to bring Ginger up-to-date on the latest episode with Jason, and her and Dan's plan.

Ginger's eyes were huge and angry by the time Jodie finished. "I can't believe he just walked into the shop like that and threatened you! What a bastard," she said a little more loudly than she should, and they both smiled, piping down as they drew a few looks.

"He is. But you know, Dan and I've decided to focus on what's more important. Us," Jodie said, feeling her cheeks turn warm.

"I told you you'd meet someone and that would be that. Your prowling days are over—the hunter has been well and truly snared," Ginger said happily.

Jodie sat back in her chair, her jaw dropping with a laugh. She was about to argue, but then her mouth clamped shut again, and she blinked.

"Yeah, I guess you were right," she said softly. "There

was only ever Dan, really." Even if she hadn't screwed up the courage to tell him so, she knew it was true.

Ginger bounced in her seat, clapping lightly, her eyes dancing. "I am so happy for you," she said. "Dan is perfect for you, and you deserve to be happy."

Jodie's cheeks warmed, but she only smiled, stabbing at her salad and changing the subject. Ginger was right, but Jodie wasn't up to having her newfound emotional life diagnosed over lunch.

"So how are things with Scott?"

Ginger's cheeks were turning pink and she appeared tentative again.

"I was going to tell you at the bakery the other day, but I guess my emotions were running really high, too. But…I think I'm pregnant. It's kind of early to know for sure, but, well, I just think I am."

Jodie dropped her fork, and the clatter distracted them both as the handsome waiter appeared at her side almost immediately with a new one.

She rolled her eyes, and they chuckled as he left, but then she met Ginger's worried gaze again.

"Pregnant? Really?" she asked.

"Yes. And…it's wonderful," Ginger said, getting misty again. "We couldn't be happier. He's been so great, Jodie. It's like something really has changed," she said, dabbing at her eyes again.

Jodie consumed the new information, processing it.

"He's happy about it?"

"Oh, yes. He's thrilled. He told me anything I want to do is fine with him. I can do whatever work I want to or not even work at all, but I love working with you at the shop. He wants to buy a house," she said, her eyes shining.

"Wow," was all Jodie could manage for a moment, and then she just shook her head. "Well, I'll say congratulations, then, and I hope you will be happy, Ginger. Because no matter what you say, you and Anna really deserve it this time around, and if Scott hurts you, tell him I'll—"

"He won't. I just know it this time," Ginger said, practically glowing with happiness.

"How do you know?"

Ginger shrugged. "I tried to get past the past, I guess. I watched him with Anna the other night and saw his face when I told him I was pregnant, and I just…know. Sometimes you just know."

Jodie was humbled. She'd been critical of Ginger, unfairly so. Love was…complicated. People did their best, and sometimes it worked out and sometimes it didn't, but Ginger at least was open to it.

"Ginger, you are probably the bravest woman I know," she said honestly. "To have faith that you could find real love, and a family, with Scott again. It's a chance I don't know that I could have taken."

Hell, she couldn't even tell Dan, whom she loved, and who clearly loved her, how she felt.

"Aw, Jodie. It's not so hard. Not when you really love someone. Like you love Dan."

"I love Dan," Jodie said on a whisper, out loud, mostly to herself, to see if she actually could form the words. Then she looked at Ginger. "I love Dan," she said again, louder and stronger, smiling.

"Question is," Ginger posed, "have you told him that?"

Jodie took a deep breath and released something that had been caught tight in her chest for a very long time. It made her feel free for the first time since…well, maybe ever.

Dan wasn't her father, and she wasn't her mother. They had a whole different relationship, and their future would be whatever they wanted it to be. Dan loved her. And she loved him.

She smiled at Ginger. "I think he suspects, but it's probably time I told him."

"Go. Do it. Now," Ginger ordered. "Lunch is on me. See you at the shop tomorrow?"

Jodie grinned, planting a kiss on Ginger's cheek as she rushed out from the restaurant.

"You bet."

Jodie rushed into Dan's office, and found him talking and laughing with a group of young people who all looked at her in surprise.

She stopped short in midstride. "Oh! I'm so sorry! I saw the door open, and I just thought—"

Dan smiled. "No problem. We're almost done here. Guys, this is my girlfriend, Jodie."

Jodie actually felt herself blush with pleasure. For a moment she thought he'd only introduce her as his business partner. Girlfriend was fine with her, and probably appropriate for the age group he was talking to. She smiled at the friendly faces.

"Hi. Sorry again for interrupting," she said to them. "The door was open, and I just assumed—"

"It's fine. Nothing top secret going on here," Dan joked, wiggling his eyebrows.

One student with blue hair and more piercings than Jodie could count gave her an appraising look and then turned to Dan.

"Nice going, Dr. Ellison," he said, making everyone chuckle, Jodie, too.

"I'll just step back out," she said, turning, but Dan shook his head, standing.

"We're pretty much done here. These guys are going to be my lab assistants this semester. We were reviewing the schedule, but we're all set, right, guys?"

"Absolutely, Dr. E," one shorter, more serious looking student said.

All three smiled and said goodbyes—to Jodie, too— and she rolled her eyes as the pierced guy threw Dan a thumbs-up on his way out.

"They're funny," Jodie said, as Dan closed the door behind them and kissed her. "Especially the pierced guy. I can tell he's always been the class clown."

"They're also incredibly smart, especially him. They'll be great to work with this term," he said. "What brings you here? Not that I'm not always glad to see you running into my office," he joked.

"Sorry again. I just got kind of excited, and I wanted to tell you something," she said, feeling her breath catch up in her chest, sudden nerves gripping her.

"Excited? About what?" Dan asked.

Jodie opened her mouth, but no sound came out.

She couldn't believe it.

At the café, with Ginger, she had been so sure that she could do this. She loved Dan. She loved him heart and soul. So why couldn't she actually say the words?

Because it wasn't about loving him. She'd loved him forever, but once she said those words, in the way he wanted to hear them, they were forever.

They'd been friends for years, but lovers only for a short time. What about when the passion faded? What if she fell short, or disappointed him or he changed his mind...what would she do then?

Her eyes drifted over the degrees and awards on the walls, his publications. The shelves of books, all of which he'd probably read. Would she be enough for him, forever? Would love be enough? She'd never been in a long-term relationship before, never thought about her future with a man—maybe marriage, a family—and all of these insecurities were new. She needed more time.

"Jodie?" Dan said, sounding more concerned. Cowardice claimed her once again, and she backed off her declaration. Maybe she would wait until they were more alone. When she could fix up her hair, make a nice dinner, turn the lights down low. This was no way to say the most important thing she ever had to say to Dan. What had she been thinking?

Searching wildly for something to say, her mind kicked up an idea. Why hadn't it occurred to her before?

She smiled ruefully. "Sorry, I was just lost in thought. It's about Jason."

Dan's brow furrowed, his expression darkening. "What did he do now?"

"Oh, no, nothing. It's more what I think we can do. I think there's a way I could get him to confess if you can still get that bug, or whatever it is. If you're willing?"

Dan stepped away, walking farther from the door, back toward his desk, motioning to her to join him.

"I thought we were done with that? I passed his proposal up to the committee with an alternate suggestion this morning, and it will take some time to hear, but…"

"You know that will never be good enough for him. What if they refuse him, anyway? He'll always hold this over our heads unless we do something to expose him. We need to get that leverage you were talking about, and I think I know how to do it."

Dan pinched the bridge of his nose, and nodded. "Okay, what did you have in mind?"

"I'll call him, ask him to meet me. I can tell him that I made a mistake, or that I'm willing to do anything for him to not hurt the business. Try to…well, you know, flirt a little and see if I can get him to confess. If he does, we'll have what we need."

Dan's frown carved deeper into his expression. "No, I don't like it. I don't want you having to do that, to get that close to him."

"Dan, I really want to. While he's blackmailing you, he's using me, and my business, to do it. You know me, Dan. You know I'm not one to sit on the sidelines," she said, convincing herself of the plan she'd thought of only seconds before.

If she and Dan had a future together, she was going to start fighting for it now. They could handle Jason, together.

Dan paused, watching her closely, then nodded. "Okay, I guess I understand how you would want to do this. But I worry about you getting hurt."

Jodie shook her head. "I don't think he's dangerous, not in the physical sense. He's slimy, but he doesn't seem like the violent type. Besides, you and your friend could be close by, anyway."

"I think you're right," he said, and started to sound excited about her plan, too. "Let me talk to Kevin. It shouldn't be difficult to set up. Meet Jason in a public place, though."

"I'll meet him at the bakery," she agreed.

"That does have a certain poetic justice to it."

She hugged him then, soaking up his scent, his warmth.

"This will work, I know it."

"I hope so," Dan said, his arms coming around and holding her close. "I really do."

13

THINGS FELL INTO PLACE more quickly than she
imagined.

The next evening, Jodie took a deep breath, squaring
her jaw and reminding herself that she was perfectly
safe. She'd felt a bit braver in Dan's office the day before, when this had been hypothetical, but now it was
all real.

Dan and his friend Kevin were just a few yards
down the street in a car, watching and listening, and
they would be in the door quickly if there was a serious
problem.

She'd called Jason from Dan's office, asked him to
meet her here at the bakery. It had taken all of her resolve to muster up a sexy enough tone to tempt him, but
she'd just looked into Dan's face and pretended she was
talking to him, instead.

Now, it was actually happening.

She didn't even feel the teensy listening device that
Dan and Kevin had taped behind the barely-there bodice
of her dress. It looked like a small mole, and wouldn't

come off even if touched. Kevin assured her he had a special remover, like for nail polish, that would take it off easily, later.

It was hard to believe the little device would pick up everything said within fifteen feet in any direction—the marvels of modern technology.

Amazing, she thought, as she considered the things that happened in Dan's world. He really did operate on a level that was different than everyone else's. But to her, he was merely the man she loved. It was killing her that she hadn't had the courage to tell him, and she wanted to remedy that very soon.

When all of this was over, she would get past this emotional block, and let him know how she felt. She made that promise to herself as she punched in the security code and then slid her key into the lock. She stepped inside, turning around to look back out at the street.

Resisting the temptation to tip her chin and speak into the bug, she said, "Can you guys hear me? Everything's working?"

She saw the headlights flash and knew that was the signal for A-okay.

"Well, he's not here yet...I guess I'll bait the trap a bit," she said, wishing Jason would show up so she could get this over with.

She took the tote bag she'd brought with her to the back, turned on one of the lights over the desk where she worked on the books, and set out a few candles, a small vase of flowers. A bottle of wine and two glasses were next, and she plucked a few of the Passionate Hearts cookies from the refrigerator, arranging them on a plate. Not that she intended on taking one bite. No way.

It was as seductive as she was willing to be in the office space of her business, but it would help get her point across. While Jason was a jerk, he was a shrewd jerk, and she had to be as convincing as possible.

She slipped her coat off and felt strangely exposed in the flirty black dress she wore—a dress clearly meant to convey to any man that she wanted him to take it off. Normally such a thing didn't bother her, but it did tonight. She wished sorely that Dan was the one she was setting the scene for, and that he would take the dress off.

Not that she had any intention of letting things go that far with Jason.

A soft knock at the front door made her jump, and she put a hand to her throat, steadying the real slamming of her pulse.

Jason waited by the door, his eyes raking up and down her body, taking in the dress, and she did her best to ignore the lascivious look. She smiled and welcomed him in, reminding herself that if she could get him to talk, she could end this all here and now. She was doing this for her and Dan, for their future, and that thought gave her confidence.

"Jason, I wasn't sure you'd come," she said, feigning relief. She closed the door behind them, only playing at locking it, and led him behind the counter, walking with a sexy sashay. She could almost feel his eyes on her backside as she did, and wrinkled her nose when he couldn't see.

"I must admit, I was surprised by your call." He held his distance. She could see in his face that while he couldn't hide his lust, he was also suspicious. His eyes traveled around the room, taking in the scene as she intended him to.

"What's this about?" he asked.

She sat on a wooden stool by the desk, and let the hem of the dress ride up higher.

"I bet you were surprised. But here's the thing. I'm a practical girl. I know that you're holding all of the cards. You could hurt the store, and frankly, I can't let that happen."

She took a breath, clenching her fingers to appear stressed and nervous—Dan told her Jason would notice such small physical cues, and they would convince him she was being sincere.

"Dan did pass your proposal to the committee, but there's no guarantee that they will approve it, either," she said, holding his look, making him believe her.

"So I decided to take things into my own hands. I...I want to make a deal with you. I'll make good on our date—one night—if you'll give back the formula and everything else you stole from the store that night of the break-in. And leave Dan alone."

Jason's eyebrows flew up. She really had surprised him, and she hoped that gave her an advantage.

"Are you saying you'd sleep with me to get that recipe?"

Jodie nodded. "Why not? I was going to sleep with you then, and we just never got around to it. Make no mistake, I'm with Dan, but I see this as helping us in the long run. Everyone gets what they want," she said huskily, leaning in as if to convince him, and letting the bodice of her dress dip provocatively.

"Dan's doing all he can," she continued, "but I need to know you won't hurt him or the store. I know you want me, Jason," she said. "And I know that having me while I'm with Dan will just make it better for you."

He smiled, his eyes mean. "That's true. But what's to stop me from telling him?"

She shrugged. "It's part of our deal that I hope you'll stick to, but it's also a risk I have to take. You were right before. Dan doesn't put anything ahead of himself, not even me. So, I guess I figured I had to do the same."

Jason nodded, stepping closer.

"I see. That's a reasonable conclusion," he said, reaching out to run his hand down her cheek, cupping her chin. "You know, if you dumped him altogether and agreed to be with me for an indefinite time, I'd make it very worth your while. Dan's not the only one with money and influence."

"Your research would never make it then."

He smiled. "It would be worth it. I could find funding elsewhere," he said dismissively.

"I never meant to put you in the middle, Jodie, but I'm also a practical person. In fact, I think you and I are a lot alike."

Jodie wanted to shudder. She never wanted that to be true.

"As I told you, I was only trying to get Dan to be fair with departmental money." He stopped, blowing out a breath. "And to be truthful, I guess I *was* jealous that you went with him and dumped me. I thought you and I had some amazing chemistry, until he came along and messed it up."

What an operator, she thought.

"Yes. I suppose." She pouted enticingly. "I'm sorry if I hurt you. But all I can offer is the one night. You give me back what you took from the bakery that night, and stop blackmailing Dan, and me, and I'll…do anything you want."

"Anything?" he asked, lifting his eyes from her breasts to her face.

Sleaze. It was only one of the names she was silently calling him in her mind as she smiled.

She shivered with repulsion from the touch on her face, his finger drifting lightly down her throat, pausing above the edge of the dress. His eyes flared with desire. She knew his ego would fill in the blanks from here on in.

Suddenly, his arms were around her, his mouth on hers. She hadn't seen that coming. She forced herself to relax, to kiss him back, but when his hand slid up her waist to her breast, she pushed him away gently, laughing, though she dearly wanted to break his fingers.

She also hoped Dan wasn't going ballistic in the car, that he let her finish this.

"Hey, hold on. I didn't hear you agreeing to my terms," she told him, holding him off at a distance.

"I can't wait for you any longer," he said, pushing her a little too roughly up against the edge of the desk behind her.

"I love that dress. I want to see what's under it."

His mouth was on hers again, forceful and skilled, but leaving her not only cold, but slightly panicked as she realized he was stronger than she thought, and quite intent on getting what he wanted. His hands were everywhere they shouldn't be, and Jodie made some play at kissing him while she figured out what to do.

She calmed herself with the thought that Dan and Kevin could be inside the shop very quickly.

"I said *wait*," she warned, pushing him with all the strength she could just as he was peeling the hem of her dress upward. "You aren't getting any of the goodies until you promise me that you won't send the information you stole from Just Eat It to any of my competitors, nor share it in any way."

He frowned, then shrugged, his eyes on her mouth. "Sure, what the hell? I have you." He smiled wickedly, adding, "And I plan to have you a lot tonight."

He moved in, kissing her neck, and she knew she needed more of a confession from him.

"How did you break in, anyway? I had a good alarm system on the building," she asked, sighing as he bit her ear though her hands were fists behind his back. "Not as good as what I have now, but—"

He moved backward, looking at her with glittering, lust-filled eyes. She saw it then—he wanted to brag. Perfect.

"That pathetic thing? A fourteen-year-old kid with basic computer-hacking skills could have broken in. It took me less than ten minutes to get in here. I'm surprised you hadn't been broken into before, honestly," he scoffed.

"But why not make it look like more of a robbery? You really messed the place up," she said, pouting.

He kissed her bottom lip, making her want to gag. "Sorry about that, but I had to make it look convincing enough for the police. No way would I take your earnings, though," he said, as if that was a saving grace. "I knew your insurance would handle the rest, and frankly the place needed some updating."

So he figured he'd done her a favor. Jodie had to stifle a laugh.

"I should have figured you'd be smart enough for something like that. It's kind of exciting," she said with an admiring smile. "Dan would never break a law," she added, baiting the trap.

"He is annoyingly strait-laced. I bet he bored you to death in bed," Jason said, taking her wrists unexpectedly, planting her hands above her head.

"But I won't," he said, pressing his hardness into her thigh, leaning in for another kiss.

Jodie gasped, about to yell for help when Jason was pulled back roughly, and she saw Dan there, fierce and standing over Jason where he'd punched him in the face, knocking him to the floor.

"DAN!" JODIE SAID, grabbing his arm as he pulled Jason up by the collar, ready to hit him again.

She'd never seen Dan so incredibly angry and rawly masculine. He was quite a sight, and it distracted the woman in her for a moment, before she stepped forward.

Her hands closed around Dan's hard upper arm,

knowing that if the timing and situation were different, she'd be ripping his clothes off by now. She definitely would be later, she promised herself.

Jason laughed, watching them as Dan released him, letting him drop down to the floor. Dan's arm closed around her tightly, his eyes dark and flashing as they met hers.

"Are you okay?"

"I'm fine, really. But…thanks," she said, shuddering and sneaking in closer. She hadn't expected things to get quite as physical as they had become, and was more than glad for Dan's interruption.

"You can't be surprised, Dan…how long did you think a hellcat like her would stick with you?" Jason said, wiping blood away from his lip, obviously still not clueing in to what was going on. "Besides, it's not what you think. I wasn't attacking your woman. She invited me here. Offered herself to me. Whatever was happening here, she was willing."

Jason stood, a malicious light in his eyes as he faced them.

Dan nodded. "I know."

Jason stilled. He was obviously confused by Dan's reaction.

"What do you mean, you know? How could you know?"

"We're going to have a talk, Jason, just you and me. But first, I think you need to listen to something."

"Ellison, what are you pulling? You're severely going to regret—"

"No, I don't think so. Listen."

Dan placed his iPod on the desk and suddenly Jason and Jodie's voices played clearly among them, silencing Jason as they all listened to a crystal-clear recording of the events that had happened since he'd come into the bakery.

Jodie felt renewed disgust as she listened, and stood closer to Dan, who hugged her in.

Jason's sallow, angular face was accented with anger, and maybe a hint of fear.

"You bitch!" he said, glaring at Jodie again. "This was a setup. I should have known."

Dan spoke up. "We have the whole thing, and in case voice isn't enough, the time signatures on the films from the security cameras that Jodie had installed should match the ones on our video, proving it's you who's mauling Jodie and willing to trade sex to cover up your other crimes."

They watched what little color was in Jason's face drain away as his eyes took note of the camera in the corner, across from the desk. "That's an intrusion of privacy. I'll fight it. I'll—"

"It's over, Jason," Dan said flatly. "The police would be very interested in this, concerning the break-in and, more important, I would be willing to let my good friend Dean Grandy have a listen. I have a feeling your academic ethics might be very deeply investigated at that point, and you might find it difficult to get any research done in the future. If you managed to stay out of jail."

Jason stared, silently seething. He was smart enough to know that they had bested him.

"Fine. I shall not reveal your stupid cookie formula

to anyone. I will erase all files today. And I would like that recording in return," he demanded.

"No problem," Dan said agreeably. "Here, you can have this one. We have others." He handed Jason the iPod.

"I suggest you start job-hunting. And I won't be offering a recommendation."

Jason, sneering, was wordless.

Dan knew they had won. He and Jodie together.

"I'll tender my resignation before the start of the new academic semester. It's far too stifling here anyway. I have felt constrained for quite some time," Jason said, floundering and unsuccessfully trying to save face.

Dan shrugged. "Well, wherever you end up, I hope it's far away. Don't ever darken our doorstep again."

Jason left, and Dan let out a long breath.

"Man," he said, checking his bruised knuckles. They were already starting to swell. "That felt great." He grinned, pulling Jodie up close.

Jodie slid her hands around his neck, and found his lips with hers.

"This is good," she announced, pressing against him. "Are you okay?" she asked, peering down at his swollen hand and bringing it to her lips.

"Yeah, though that's the first time I've ever had to punch anyone," he admitted. "Maybe the caveman isn't so far below my surface."

"I kind of like it when you allow your baser instincts to come out and play," she quipped. Suddenly all the props she had arranged for Jason took on a new glow, and her heart raced for Dan.

All she wanted was for him to touch her. Now. Here. Everywhere.

She desperately needed him to get rid of any memory of Jason's disgusting hands and mouth on her, and replace them with his own.

Dan seemed to know, without her saying anything.

"I'm fine. Better than fine," he assured her, leaving gentle kisses all over her face until he claimed her lips in a deeper kiss, slipping his hand into the bodice of the dress, and ripping it down the front.

"Wow," she whispered breathlessly. She really did like his caveman instincts.

"Hope that wasn't a favorite," he said, tossing the scrap to the floor, taking her in.

"Nope. That was perfect. Uh, wait...the bug?" She pointed to the mole, grinning. Dan's friend was about to get more of an earful.

"Oh, right," Dan said, laughing. "Just a second."

He dashed from the store, and was back in less than two minutes, a small bottle in his hand. He locked the door behind him, and looked at her with clear intent.

"I can remove that and get it to Kevin tomorrow. He's gone. We're alone," Dan assured her, removing the small device with the edge of a Q-tip and placing it carefully in a small metal box.

"Now," he said, "let's break a few health codes. That dangerous enough for you?" he asked, referring to her comment about him not wanting to break the law.

She grinned, already feeling lighter than she had in days, her hands finding him, making him dizzy with her touch.

"Absolutely," she replied, undressing him as his hands stripped away her undergarments. "But those security cameras are still running. They feed to a computer on my desk at home. So we can take out the recording and watch it later, maybe," she said naughtily.

"I like that idea," he agreed as she sat in a chair and he fell to his knees in front of her, kissing up the inside of her thigh and finding the hot, sweet spot that made her cry out.

Jodie looked up into the camera, making sure that every bit of her reaction to what he was doing to her as he lifted her legs over his shoulders, opening her completely, would be clear.

As he explored, and loved her with his mouth and hands, driving her to the edge, she silently mouthed the words she hoped to say to him one day soon, so that when he watched the tape at some later date, he'd know how she was feeling, even then.

14

SHE WAS LATE.

Dan watched the door, hoping Jodie made it in time. It was almost time to start. Everyone was taking seats, the Dean's voice booming out an introduction.

He knew that she'd been caught up late at the bakery, and said she would meet him here as soon as she could. He'd told her not to worry about it. She'd probably find his presentation boring anyway, and if she made it in time for the reception, that's all that mattered.

Still, he really would have loved to look out into the small audience and have seen her there. She had her business to run, and he had a paper to deliver. There would be other times, he thought reasonably, yet couldn't stop his eyes from drifting to the door as it was almost time to start.

Focusing, he took the podium and started to speak.

Just a few minutes later, she arrived. He flubbed a line, he was so taken by her. Blindingly gorgeous in a new dress, a deep blue satin that saturated her eyes with color and made her skin appear like porcelain, he completely forgot where he was and hastened to continue as people whispered, following the direction of his gaze and smiling.

Jodie smiled, mouthing a silent apology and quickly took her seat as he picked up where he left off, feeling more engaged and enthusiastic about his presentation, and soon he was as taken with the topic as his audience seemed to be. His new research was exciting, although not as exciting as the new woman in his life. He wanted to get to the end, so he could be with her.

It wasn't a surprise to him anymore that his feelings for her overrode everything, even his work. It felt right.

She had been listening attentively and looked interested in his work. Dan pushed down his impatience for this event to be over, and turned his attention to the question-and-answer session.

A man he didn't recognize at all stood up to ask a question, and Dan nodded in his direction.

"Dr. Ellison, is it true you are the mastermind behind the erotic frosting formula that is sold at Old Town's Just Eat It bakery?"

Dan paused in surprise. This had nothing to do with his presentation. The guy had to be a reporter.

"If you have a question relevant to the discussion, I'd be glad to answer," Dan said calmly. "But anything else is not up for discussion at this time."

"So, you create a groundbreaking formula that allows women to get any man they want sexually interested in them, and you don't want people to know? I mean, Dr.

Ellison, this is pretty big stuff—why don't you want people to know?"

The reporter wasn't going to give up, and security obviously hadn't been called. Everyone was murmuring, and he locked eyes with Jodie, unsure what to do. He concluded that the best course of action was the truth.

"It's true. I'm involved in several commercial endeavors in my free time," he emphasized, so that no one would think he was using university funding for his work, "and several years ago, just out of college, I did create a harmless, vegetable extract that increases women's pheromone presence slightly. We use this extract in icing for cookies at the bakery we co-own. If a woman is attracted to a certain male, not just any man, her enhanced pheromone level can potentially affect his response. As long as he is attracted to her, as well."

The reporter nodded. "So, for the formula to work, the woman has to be interested, and so does the man?"

Dan nodded. "That's pretty much the gist of it."

"So if they are already interested, what's the point of the formula?"

Dan looked at Jodie. "A lot of people have trouble expressing their emotions. They keep their desires and attractions a secret, and that could mean they lose out on the love of a lifetime. This might help them make that first move," he said.

Continuing, he added, "Most humans put out pheromone signatures on some level, but what attracts people to each other is more than physical, more than chemical. There's a complicated mix of emotional, social and psychological elements that figure into even basic physical attraction. You can't create a formula for love, I'm afraid," he said with a sheepish smile, glad to see that several people were nodding, even smiling.

"Love just happens," he added very unscientifically, smiling at Jodie, who smiled back, and then stood up. He wondered what she was about to do.

"May I say something?" she asked the room.

Dan took her in and nodded, without saying a word.

"I'm not a scientist. I only understood parts and pieces of what was discussed here tonight, but I understand the importance of the work Dr. Ellison is doing. That's what we should be talking about," she gently chastised the reporter. "However, as the owner of the bakery you're all talking about, I have to speak up."

She took a deep breath, and Dan didn't think she'd ever been more beautiful.

"Dan's formula helped me make my business a success. But more than that, all of his science is about helping people. As it turned out, his formula also helps people all the time, to have a little more confidence, a little more fun, a little more spark in their lives. For the life of me, I can't figure out why anyone would find something wrong with that," she said, again glaring directly at the reporter.

Dan discreetly covered his smile with his hand. He didn't need to say anything. Jodie was on a roll.

"And one final thing. I know the cookies have an effect, whether it's a chemical one or a psychological one, it doesn't matter."

"How do you know this?" the reporter interjected.

Jodie pulled herself up, looking so stunningly gorgeous that Dan couldn't take his eyes away from her. She looked at the reporter as she spoke.

"Because I've experienced their effect, firsthand. They helped me find the man I love. At first I thought it was just a chemical reaction, but guess what? When the effect of the frosting wears off, the feelings don't. The cookies just gave us the boost we needed to do something about it, like Dr. Ellison said. Sometimes we just need a little help expressing them, that's all."

The man I love. The words echoed in Dan's ears, and the room fell away. People murmured among themselves as he left the podium to walk to where Jodie stood, as the reporter scribbled notes frantically.

The Dean might have said something, and people were talking amongst themselves, and asking him more questions, but Dan didn't care about any of it.

He took Jodie's hand and pulled her outside where he could get her alone.

JODIE HURRIED ALONG after Dan, her heels clicking on the pavement.

"Dan! You can't just leave! This is your event," Jodie objected as they made their way across the parking lot to sit on a bench under a swaying willow tree.

"I don't care about that," he said, pulling her down on the bench with him.

Jodie's heart was beating like mad, and she was sure it wasn't from the race across the parking lot. She bit her lip.

"I'm sorry. I really did it, didn't I? Standing up and

going off like that? I didn't mean to embarrass you, but that reporter just got under my skin and—"

He put a finger to her lips. "Jodie, you could never embarrass me. I loved what you had to say. One part in particular. I was kind of hoping you could repeat it for me," he said, his hands firm and warm around hers.

Jodie's heart really did pick up speed now.

She knew what he meant, and pulled her hands from his, framing his face. She'd known this face for a long time and had never realized until now how precious this man was to her. Or maybe she had known it all along, but now she was ready to say so.

"I love you Dan. I love you so much it's almost more than I can bear. I want you, and to have a life with you, and everything that we can have together," she said.

The happiness that transformed his features touched her heart. He looked like she'd just handed him the moon, sun and stars all in one. It choked her up that anyone could feel this way about her, but especially her best friend.

"I love you, too, Jodie, and you have no idea how long I've waited to hear you say that. I want to share everything with you, too. I want to make you as happy as you've made me," he said earnestly.

Tears flowed down over tender kisses that quickly turned hot, and Dan pulled back, wiping a tear from her cheek.

"Hey, what's this?"

Jodie swallowed hard. "It just hit me, how stupid I've been for so long, when we could have been together. I've been so worried that I wouldn't be enough for you. That after the passion wore off, there wouldn't be anything else about me that interested you."

"Jodie, I have to insist on one rule in our life together," Dan said seriously, his eyes intent on hers.

"What?"

"You are never, ever, to use the word *stupid,* or any of its synonyms, in reference to yourself again. Okay? I can't have you talking about the woman I love that way because she happens to be one of the smartest, most creative, passionate, incredible people I know. I'll be happy to remind you, every day. Every night," he said huskily, leaning in for a kiss but stopping before contact. "Promise."

She smiled, laughing as more happy tears flowed. "Okay. I promise," she said, promising that and everything else she could give him.

"Good. You could never bore me. If anything, I'm the boring one," he said as he nuzzled her. "You're gorgeous, sexy and amazing. I never imagined you could feel this way about *me.*"

After long heated moments sealing the deal with kisses and touches that threatened to put the bench to very creative use, Jodie pulled away.

"Hey," Dan objected.

She shook her head. "We need to go back in. There are people waiting for you in there. I bought this dress for you—let's go celebrate."

He smiled, leaning in to kiss her again. "Okay. You're right. Besides, I want to show you off. And there are some people I'd like you to meet."

"Hmm," she said. "I've probably ruined all my makeup."

"You're perfect. But get used to it, because I have a lot of these kinds of things," he said, "and I always want you with me, by my side. I loved looking out and seeing you there tonight. It meant the world to me."

"I wouldn't have missed it," she told him, ready to face anything with Dan. "I'm so proud of you, and your work."

"As I am of you," he returned sincerely. "When we get home, we can celebrate without the dress."

Jodie smiled and stood, holding her hand out to him. So this was what it was like to be in love with a genius.

Epilogue

"GINGER, YOU SIT DOWN for a while. You shouldn't be on your feet so much," Jodie said, directing her friend to the kitchen to sit, while she waited on the seemingly never ending parade of customers.

"I'm fine. The exercise is good for me," Ginger objected, but still did as she was told, taking a seat.

"You just look a bit tired, is all," Jodie said gently. "But happy."

"You, too."

Jodie grinned. "Yeah, but I've been missing sleep for an entirely different reason."

She and Dan had been married the week before, three months after the evening of his presentation. They'd had a wonderful wedding with just their friends and family as they'd negotiated around both of their busy work schedules. But now the holiday rush was almost past, and the semester was over, and they were nearly free to spend all of their time together.

Business was booming. The reporter who'd come to the presentation was so taken with their story, he'd done a huge feature, focusing on the bakery. After the story hit the papers and they appeared on some local talk shows, answering questions about how Dan and Jodie met, the cookie icing formula and their wedding, Jodie couldn't make Passionate Hearts fast enough.

Life was good. Better than good.

Dan had never had to use the recording they had against Jason. After what had happened that night, Jason had quietly resigned and left the university. Neither she nor Dan had any idea where he was and didn't care. Good riddance, Jodie thought.

"Just you wait. Your turn is coming, you keep this up," Ginger warned with a grin.

"You need to be more careful with those predictions of yours," she teased. "I'm barely used to being married let alone have a family yet."

It had been Ginger, after all, who told her that her playgirl lifestyle would one day come crashing to a halt, and thankfully, it had.

"I'm just saying…things happen," Ginger teased.

"I know, but don't rush me. We just got hitched. I want to enjoy being us for a while."

"Don't blame you one bit," Ginger said. "I can't wait until this baby is out and Scott and I can get back to normal life, whatever that is."

"No one deserves it more."

Ginger had stopped her work at the hospital, for now anyway, and was helping full-time at the bakery as Jodie's assistant manager. She'd be taking care of the place while Jodie was out of town for the next month.

The bell over the door rang, and Jodie turned to find

Make Your Move

Scott entering the shop. No doubt he was here to take Ginger to her doctor's appointment. Dan filed in right behind him.

The four had become good friends. Ginger always teased her about getting pregnant soon so that their kids could grow up together, but Jodie knew that she really wasn't ready for that now. Her business and Dan were more than enough.

She had gotten in touch with her mother for the wedding, and it had been a healing thing. Dan had been there for her, as always, and Jodie was trying to understand her mother's choices, and to find a new kind of relationship with her. It was nice.

Still, it was her relationship with her new husband that she wanted to focus on.

"Hey, wife," he said, walking behind the counter and slipping his arms around her.

"Hey husband," she said. It was how they'd been playfully referring to each other all week.

Ginger and Scott quickly said their goodbyes and were on their way.

"Two days and counting," Dan said lustily, seeking a hot kiss that took her over so completely she didn't even hear when the bell rang again.

When she closed the shop on Sunday, they'd be leaving on their slightly delayed honeymoon to Europe. A solid month of nothing but her, Dan and enjoying every minute of their time together.

She'd been buying lingerie and special, sexy toys to bring with her since they'd started planning the trip. If airport security checked her bag, they were going to find several sexy surprises, she thought with a grin.

She and Dan had a lot of lost time to make up for.

"Do you think you two newlyweds could part long enough to sell me my cookies?" asked Mrs. Mitchell, her ever-faithful customer. The older woman's eyes sparkled with humor, as Jodie slipped away from Dan.

"Absolutely, Mrs. Mitchell. I even have something special for you today."

Jodie went to the back and brought out the box of cookies that Mrs. Mitchell had ordered, and handed them to her with a small gift bag. The woman looked in the bag, pulling out a small bottle.

"Men's cologne?" she asked curiously.

"It's Dan's formula—for men. That's a special pre-market bottle, available only to regular customers who buy Passionate Hearts. It won't hit the shelf for another few weeks. I think you'll like it," Jodie said with a wink.

Mrs. Mitchell's eyes lit up, and she shook her head, laughing. "Well, maybe we'll have a bit of a honeymoon this month, too! You kids enjoy yourselves," she said, heading back out, obviously excited to go home and give it a try.

"Oh, don't worry, we will," Jodie said, flipping the sign to Closed and locking the door. She eyed Dan seductively and pulled the string on her apron.

Dan watched appreciatively as she discarded the apron, then started unbuttoning her blouse, walking toward him with clear intention. "Want to break a few more of those health codes?" she asked playfully.

"Don't you have a few more hours until you close up?"

"I don't want to wait another day to get this honeymoon started," she said, leading him into the back room.

"But what about your customers?" he said against her lips.

She smiled. "They'll understand," she said, slipping the shirt off. "I need a little energy boost," she said sexily.

He didn't argue, reaching around to unclasp her bra, filling his hands with her breasts. Jodie sighed then moaned as he touched her in all the ways she loved and that never stopped turning her on. Dan turned her on more than anyone ever had, ever would.

"I love you, Dan," she said earnestly, as he took her breath away with his touch.

"I love you, too," he whispered against her skin, and Jodie knew she'd never get tired of hearing it, or saying it. Though right now, they had better things to do than talk.

Harlequin offers a romance for every mood!
See below for a sneak peek
from our suspense romance line
Silhouette® Romantic Suspense.
Introducing HER HERO IN HIDING by
New York Times *bestselling author Rachel Lee.*

Kay Young returned to woozy consciousness to find that she was lying on a soft sofa beneath a heap of quilts near a cheerfully burning fire. When she tried to move, however, everything hurt, and she groaned.

At once she heard a sound, then a stranger with a hard, harsh face was squatting beside her. "Shh," he said softly. "You're safe here. I promise."

"I have to go," she said weakly, struggling against pain. "He'll find me. He can't find me."

"Easy, lady," he said quietly. "You're hurt. No one's going to find you here."

"He will," she said desperately, terror clutching at her insides. "He always finds me!"

"Easy," he said again. "There's a blizzard outside. No one's getting here tonight, not even the doctor. I know, because I tried."

"Doctor? I don't need a doctor! I've got to get away."

"There's nowhere to go tonight," he said levelly. "And if I thought you could stand, I'd take you to a window and show you."

But even as she tried once more to pull away the quilts, she remembered something else: this man had been gentle when he'd found her beside the road, even when she had kicked and clawed. He hadn't hurt her.

Terror receded just a bit. She looked at him and detected signs of true concern there.

The terror eased another notch and she let her head sag on the pillow. "He always finds me," she whispered.

"Not here. Not tonight. That much I can guarantee."

Will Kay's mysterious rescuer protect
her from her worst fears?
Find out in HER HERO IN HIDING
by New York Times bestselling author Rachel Lee.
Available June 2010, only from
Silhouette® Romantic Suspense.

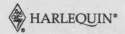

Silhouette *Desire*

From *USA TODAY* bestselling author

LEANNE BANKS

CEO'S EXPECTANT SECRETARY

Elle Linton is hiding more than just her affair
with her boss Brock Maddox. And she's
terrifed that if their secret turns public her
mother's life may be put at risk. When she
unexpectedly becomes pregnant she's forced
to make a decision. Will she be able to save
her relationship and her mother's life?

*Available June
wherever books are sold.*

Always Powerful, Passionate and Provocative.

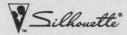

HARLEQUIN® Romance®

GIRLS' Weekend in VEGAS

Four friends, four dream weddings!

On a girly weekend in Las Vegas, best friends Alex, Molly,
Serena and Jayne are supposed to just have fun and forget
men, but they end up meeting their perfect matches!
Will the love they find in Vegas stay in Vegas?

Find out in this sassy, fun and wildly romantic miniseries
all about love and friendship!

Saving Cinderella! by MYRNA MACKENZIE
Available June

Vegas Pregnancy Surprise by SHIRLEY JUMP
Available July

Inconveniently Wed! by JACKIE BRAUN
Available August

Wedding Date with the Best Man
by MELISSA MCCLONE
Available September

REQUEST YOUR FREE BOOKS!

2 FREE NOVELS PLUS 2 FREE GIFTS!

HARLEQUIN®

Blaze

Red-hot reads!

HB10R

Love Inspired

Bestselling author

JILLIAN HART

brings you another heartwarming story
from

the
GRANGER
FAMILY
RANCH

Rancher Justin Granger hasn't seen his high school sweetheart since she rode out of town with his heart. Now she's back, with sadness in her eyes, seeking a job as his cook and housekeeper. He agrees but is determined to avoid her...until he discovers that her big dream has always been him!

The Rancher's Promise

*Available June
wherever books are sold.*

Steeple
Hill®
LI87601